LUCKY ESCAPE

LUCKY BREAK SERIES
BOOK 4

HOPE MALONE

Paperback ISBN: 978-1-991321-25-1

For information regarding permission to use excerpts in reviews, email the author at thebirds@thepapersparrow.com subject line: Permission

ONE

MALAKAI

The old Donovan warehouse sat brooding over the Coogan's Break historic district, a forgotten monument to California's gold rush days. In running my hand along the rough-hewn blocks, I could feel the hard graft that had gone into this place. Its stone walls, while weathered, were still solid after more than a century and a half, harking back to a time when things were built to last.

Ethan Hunter, my boss and the owner of Lucky Break Construction, joined me at the base of the building. "What do you think, Mal?" His practiced eye was already cataloging structural issues, the way mine scanned for security vulnerabilities.

"Good bones," I admitted, though my attention

kept drifting to the sounds coming from inside the warehouse. Footsteps, the scrape of something heavy being moved, and what might have been cursing in a feminine voice.

"The owner's already here," said Daemon, checking his watch. "We're right on time." This was something of a miracle when it came to Daemon, with his dating proclivities regularly seeing him stuck in bed. Often because he'd been handcuffed to the headboard.

Tyler nodded toward the main entrance. "Should we knock, or just head in?"

Before anyone could answer, the question became moot. The heavy wooden door swung open, and I forgot how to breathe. Sure, I'd had a look around the woman's website just out of habit, but nothing could have prepared me for the vision confronting me.

She was covered in dust from head to toe, with streaks through her long, dark hair, smudges across her cheeks, and what looked like a century of grime coating her faded jeans and a t-shirt that was just as filthy. She should have looked like a mess.

Instead, all I could think about was how much I wanted to clean her up.

Take my time.

Use my tongue.

Christ, where the hell had that come from?

Damn it, the last thing I needed in my life was a

distraction as gorgeous as this one. Any loss of focus wouldn't just affect me; it could affect those around me, including her.

"You must be the Lucky Break team," she said, wiping her hands on a rag that was doubtless dirtier than her palms. "I'm Amelia Donovan. Sorry, I'm a mess, but I was trying to get a proper look at the layout before you arrived."

She extended a hand toward Ethan, and I watched her move with an unconscious grace that made my mouth go dry. There was something about her confidence, the way she owned this space despite looking like she'd been wrestling with it, that hit me right in the gut. Her open expression told me she'd never had to hide from anything or anyone in her life.

And if that weren't enough, she was all woman with curves aplenty. Perhaps it was because I was a bit of a unit myself, but I liked a woman with some meat on her bones. No chance of my breaking her when things get heated.

When things get heated? Don't you mean if, *Mal?*

Sheesh, the very thought was enough to have me shoving my hands in my pockets for fear I'd give myself away.

"Ethan Hunter," said my very married boss, shaking her hand without seeming to care about the dust transfer. "This is Daemon, Tyler, and Malakai."

When she turned those dark eyes on me, I felt the impact like a physical blow. "Malakai Torres," I managed, relieved that my greeting came out steady.

Her handshake was firm, no-nonsense, but I caught myself holding on a beat longer than necessary. Her skin was soft and warm beneath the grime, and I had to fight the urge to stroke my thumb across her knuckles.

Get a grip, Torres. You're not in a position to be thinking about anything more than casual, and there's nothing casual about this woman.

"So," said Ethan, breaking the moment, "I've seen your plans, but perhaps you'd like to tell us about your vision for the place."

Amelia's face lit up, and the dust no longer mattered. She was beautiful when passionate, her hands moving as she described her plans for converting the warehouse into a mixed-use development. Something meaningful that was all about creation rather than destruction.

"I want to keep the historical integrity while making it earthquake safe," she explained, leading us through the cavernous main floor. "Artists' studios and maker spaces down here, loft apartments upstairs. The stone construction is solid, but I know we'll need to bring everything up to current seismic standards."

Ethan nodded, already pulling out his tablet to make notes. "These stone walls will handle the retrofit work, but we'll need to assess the internal support structure." He looked up at the exposed beams overhead. "I'm thinking steel reinforcement, modern anchoring systems. It's doable, but it won't be cheap."

"I figured as much," said Amelia. "This place has been in my family for generations, but it's been sitting empty for decades. I decided it was time either to accept one of the offers or to do something with the place."

"There's someone interested in buying?" I asked, unable to keep the surprise out of my voice. While the place might have good bones, it was one hell of an undertaking, especially when you considered the historic-preservation covenant the city's planning department had just slapped on the place.

That this little piece of red tape hadn't been there when Ethan was contacted about the job was enough to have my instincts pinging. Something felt off, though I couldn't put my finger on what.

"Yes," said Amelia. "There have been inquiries for years, but they've picked up of late. Nothing aggressive, just persistent." She shrugged. "But I'm not interested in selling. This place has too much history. Family history."

I filed that information away. Persistent buyers and additional hoops to jump through right when she was ready to start the renovation? Might be a coincidence. But it might also be something else.

As we moved through the building, I let the others focus on construction issues while I did what I did best. Assess threats and general security. The warehouse had too many entry points, windows at ground level, and sight lines that would be a challenge for off-the-shelf security equipment. But it wasn't just the building that had my attention.

We were being watched.

There was that familiar prickle between my shoulder blades that had saved my life more times than I could count during my government days. The spike in my cortisol was just as it had been back then, too.

Damn it, I'd been so careful, never making too much noise, keeping within society's guidelines, always playing the part. And for what, to have some asshole pin me now. It was something that had me looking anywhere but at Amelia.

If someone from my old life thought they could get to me through her, they wouldn't think twice. And if they thought that, they'd find out the hard way that I wouldn't back down in protecting the innocent.

A sideways glance through the rippled glass of a large window to the street beyond told me that whoever they were, they weren't complete amateurs. If they had been, my experience was such that I'd have spotted them.

"The top floor has amazing potential," said Amelia as we climbed the stairs. "I'm thinking of two-bedroom lofts with exposed brick and steel. Maybe six units total."

I tuned back in, forcing myself to focus on the conversation while keeping part of my awareness on our surroundings. The woman knew her stuff, with every detail she mentioned showing careful thought and genuine passion for historical preservation.

"What's your timeline?" asked Daemon.

"I was hoping to start construction within the month," said Amelia. "The architectural plans are complete, and I'm expecting permits from the city any day now. I just need a contractor I can trust to do this right."

As if on cue, there was a brief knock at the main door below. We all froze in response, listening as the initial knock was backed up with sharp, official-sounding raps. Whoever it was meant business. Could this be who I'd sensed earlier?

No, that made no sense. For one thing, people from my past never announced their presence. Anything but.

"Were you expecting someone?" asked Ethan, knowing as I did that everyone else from Lucky Break was busy on a home renovation on the other side of town.

Amelia shook her head, already heading for the stairs. "No, but I'd better see who it is."

We followed her back to the first floor, and I was unsure what to focus on. The way Amelia's ass looked in those jeans or the sinking sensation in my gut brought on by someone showing up unannounced.

Experience told me coincidences were often anything but, and that right when we were discussing permits, there was a knock at the door. The timing was too convenient for me to be okay with it.

Amelia opened the door to reveal a small weasel of a man in an ill-fitting suit, clipboard in hand and wearing an expression that screamed bureaucratic authority. However, when he saw Ethan, Tyler, Daemon, and me, his attitude dropped a notch.

It even looked like he was about to bolt, but after a glance over his shoulder, he stepped forward. "Ms. Donovan? I'm Howard Pruitt from city planning. I'm here about your renovations."

"Okay," said Amelia, the word drawn out. "But the permits have already been submitted, and I've been told they're under review."

Pruitt made a show of consulting his clipboard. "Yes, well, that's what I'm here about. There seem to be some... complications with your application."

I stepped closer, my protective instincts flaring. There was something about this guy's manner that set my teeth on edge, the way his eyes darted around, taking in everything while pretending to focus on the paperwork attached to his clipboard.

"What complications?" asked Ethan, his voice carrying the edge of someone who'd dealt with city planning officials before.

"Seismic retrofit requirements, that sort of thing," said Pruitt, addressing Ethan while shooting nervous glances at me and Tyler. "For a structure of this age and size, we're looking at extensive modifications. Steel reinforcement, complete strengthening of the foundations, updated electrical and plumbing to modern codes. I'd estimate you're looking at additional costs in the many hundreds of thousands."

"The foundations?" Amelia's voice climbed. "I saw nothing in the building codes that would imply they needed work."

Pruitt shrugged with practiced indifference. "Regulations change, Ms. Donovan. Safety is our primary concern." Then, not giving Amelia a chance to respond, he again focused on his paperwork as if searching for further obstacles.

While he did so, I studied the man's body language, looking for chinks in his armor. I found them soon enough in the way he was avoiding eye contact, how his hands shook as he flipped through his papers. He was lying, or he'd expected Amelia to be on her own.

"Could we get that assessment in writing?" I asked, stepping into his line of sight as I'd have done without thinking in my old life, anything to protect the asset. Except this wasn't a contract; this was personal.

As close as I now was to the odious little bureaucrat, he had no option but to look up at me, something that had me standing even taller. "With specific code citations and engineering requirements?" I added only after he'd looked me in the eye.

While I might not have been up to speed with building codes, I understood all too well how paper pushers in government departments worked.

The effect was immediate. Pruitt took a half-step back, his Adam's apple bobbing as he swallowed hard. "I... well, that is... the full report will be available once the review committee has completed its assessment."

"And when will that be?" pressed Amelia.

"Hard to say. These things take time. Could be weeks, could be months," he said, taking another step back. "I just wanted to give you a heads-up about potential pitfalls. No point in proceeding if the numbers don't work for you."

He appeared ready to add another impediment when a car horn began blaring outside. Long, insistent honks followed by a series of short blasts that echoed off the warehouse walls.

As unexpected as the noise was in this quiet part of town, was watching Pruitt's reaction, with his face paling, and beads of sweat popping up on his top lip.

"I... I have to go," he stammered, all pretense of official authority evaporating, the sniffling little creep showing himself out soon after.

Despite this, the horn continued its demanding chorus, with Ethan and me moving to the nearest window to see what was up. It was a move that saw us blocking Amelia's view when she tried to peer around us.

"That's an interesting car for a government employee," observed Ethan. "Old but in mint condition. The guy didn't strike me as a car fanatic."

"What are you on about?" Amelia asked, still trying to get a clear look.

"Your planning department friend's driving an eighties sedan that looks to be straight out of the showroom," I said over my shoulder. "Older woman in the passenger seat, silver hair. She appears pissed he's taking too long. She's the one leaning on the horn."

Through the cacophony, Pruitt wrenched open the driver's door of the dark sedan, bringing the noise to an abrupt stop.

"How old is she?" asked Amelia. "Like, are we

talking 'take your grandmother to work day' or just a senior employee?" She'd then backed this up with, "Let me see."

But by the time Ethan moved to the side to give her a clear view, the sedan had already pulled away with a screech of tires. Not that my mind was on that. With Amelia now peering out the window next to me, her perfume was wafting and tickling my nostrils. Well, them, and other parts of me further south.

"What the hell was that all about?" muttered Tyler, waving his hand around the warehouse. This confirmed to me he wasn't talking about the visit in general, but rather the asshat's strange departure.

Ethan ran a hand through his hair. "I'd say that was someone trying to scare Amelia off this project."

"But why?" she asked, genuine confusion in her voice.

"That's a good question," I said, turning to look back out the window, wondering if I'd see Pruitt and his mystery passenger come back this way. "And I think we need the answer."

"You think he was lying about the requirements?" asked Amelia.

"I think he's talking bullshit," said Ethan from behind us, his words blunt. "This place is a qualified historical building under the State Historical Building Code. Don't get me wrong, you'll need seismic upgrades, but there's no need to go to the expense of shoring up the foundations. Not with a building as solid as this one."

Relief washed over Amelia's face. "So, this is still doable?"

"Hell yes," Ethan confirmed. " We're talking maybe fifty, sixty thousand for a retrofit, not several hundred. The question is why someone wants you to think it isn't." After a quick scan of the central atrium, he again looked at Amelia. "Even so, we'll need to be all over costs and timelines to avoid any overruns."

As I wondered about Pruitt's surprise visit and his attempts to stonewall Amelia, my mind was already working through possibilities. Someone had been trying to buy this property. Someone who might have connections in city planning. What if the same individual were prepared to manufacture obstacles to force a sale?

I stared out the window for a moment longer, running through everything in my head before turning to face Amelia. "Those offers to buy this place, were they local?"

She shook her head before answering. "I'm not sure. The offers always came through a lawyer, and when I asked who was interested in buying, I was told it was confidential."

She paused, as if remembering something. "When I

think about it, there was one time, maybe five years ago, when my great-aunt was still alive. She mentioned that some woman—a Maggie Pearson—had cornered her at the grocery store. Very polite, very proper, but persistent questions about whether our family might ever consider selling."

"Maggie Pearson?" My voice sharpened.

"My great-aunt said she remembered her from when they were young. Apparently, Maggie's from a prominent founding family, or something. But Aunt Rose said she was always a bit ... intense." Amelia paused, then added, "Intense enough that she's on husband number three by all accounts."

After tidying my mustache without much thought, I asked her the other thing that was bothering me. "Has anyone in the planning department contacted you before today?"

Again, Amelia shook her head. "All my dealings have been through the main office. I've never heard of this Pruitt guy."

"I'll check him out," I said. "See if he's even legit."

She turned to study me, those dark eyes seeing more than I wanted them to. "You think there's something wrong here."

It wasn't a question, and I respected her for not pretending this was normal.

"I think someone doesn't want you to renovate this

building," I admitted. "And I think they're willing to play dirty to stop you."

Next to us, Ethan stood staring up at the heavy wooden beams high overhead, not bothering to change his stance when he spoke. "So what do we do about it?"

Amelia straightened her shoulders, and I saw steel beneath the dust and femininity. "For starters, we move forward with anything that doesn't require a permit. If someone thinks they can intimidate me into giving up my family's building, they're about to learn otherwise."

The fierce determination in her voice did something to me, something that went beyond physical attraction, and back to a time when I'd have had no reason to hide my response.

This woman had backbone, intelligence, and the stubborn courage that got under a man's skin. It was the sort that drew me in, the drive to protect as strong as it had been since before my life went off the rails.

I'd seen female agents display the same traits back in the day. What they'd lacked in physical strength, they'd more than made up for in raw intelligence and street cunning. Hadn't I learned the hard way not to underestimate that?

And all of that was why I needed to be careful around this gorgeous woman. I wasn't Malakai Torres, an upstanding citizen who could offer someone like her the future she deserved. I was a ghost, dead for all intents and purposes, with a past that could get her killed if the wrong people came looking.

But as I watched her survey her family's warehouse with plans and dreams shining in her eyes, I knew it was already too late for careful.

I was in trouble. Big trouble. The sort to compromise my cover and my self-imposed isolation.

But for the first time in years, I wasn't sure I wanted to fight it.

TWO

AMELIA

I watched the Lucky Break crew drive away from the warehouse, my mind still reeling from the encounter with Howard Pruitt. More than that, I was trying to process my reaction to Malakai Torres.

The man was trouble with a capital T, and I was smart enough to recognize it. The way he'd moved through the warehouse, with his dark eyes missing nothing. Then there was that crazy ringmaster mustache of his, with its handlebar perfection, that somehow suited him to a T.

In the past, I'd have found this a turnoff, as it was, just thinking about it was enough to have me imagining him wielding a whip and ordering me about. Would I take direction from him and enjoy it? The tingling at the apex of my thighs told me that was a definitive yes.

After shaking my head to clear it of these dirty thoughts, I focused on the protective way he'd stepped between me and that slimy planning official. While there was something about Malakai that screamed danger, rather than wanting to escape his orbit, I wanted to get closer. A lot closer.

Which was unlike me. I was the sensible one, the woman who planned everything down to the last detail and never made impulsive decisions. Except for this warehouse renovation, of course.

The thought brought me up short. When had I started making exceptions? The warehouse project itself had been my first real deviation from the careful path I'd mapped out for my life. A successful architecture career, a predictable routine, relationships that never demanded too much or risked too little. Safe. Controlled.

But also increasingly boring.

Standing here in this crumbling building, feeling drawn to a dangerous man with secrets in his eyes, I was wondering if "sensible" had become just another word for "afraid."

I leaned against the stone wall and let myself think about the building that had been haunting my family for generations. Growing up, I'd heard the stories about great-great-grandfather Jeremiah Donovan and his gold rush fortune.

How he'd built this warehouse to store supplies for the miners, and how he'd made and lost a fortune. Perhaps the saddest aspect of Jeremiah's life was how he'd apparently died in assisted living, subsisting on gray food, and raving about hidden gold.

My great-grandmother used to tell those tales with such drama, making Jeremiah out to be everything from a saint to a scoundrel depending on her mood. My father had been more practical about it, dismissing most of the stories as family legend that had grown with each telling.

"It's just a building, Amelia," he used to say when I urged him to renovate. "I won't let the family ghost stories cloud my judgment. Nor should you."

But standing there, I could sense the family legacy within these walls. This place had been built during one of the most exciting times in California's history, when fortunes were made and lost overnight, when desperate men traveled thousands of miles chasing dreams of gold.

More than that, I was questioning everything about the careful life I'd built. When had I become so focused on avoiding risk that I'd stopped taking chances on anything meaningful? My business was successful but predictable. My relationships had been safe but unsatisfying. Even this warehouse project was the first real leap of faith I'd taken in years.

Standing in this building that had witnessed decades of dreams and disappointments, I wondered if my great-great-grandfather Jeremiah had played it safe. The stories suggested he'd been a risk-taker, a man who'd bet everything on his vision and built something lasting.

Maybe it was time I stopped jumping at my own shadow and started trying to become more like him. To chase something. Not gold, but the person I used to be before I'd let caution calcify into fear.

The girl who'd dreamed of creating something meaningful, before I'd settled for designing other people's visions because it was safer than risking my own.

The warehouse renovation wasn't just about honoring Jeremiah's legacy. It was about reclaiming mine.

The irony wasn't lost on me that someone was still chasing those dreams, still trying to buy this property even after all this time.

The first offer I was aware of had come when I was in college, just after my grandfather died and left the warehouse to my father. A modest sum with no explanation of why anyone would want a crumbling building in a town only just hanging onto its tourist trade.

My father had turned it down without much thought. However, the offers kept coming, every few years like clockwork. The other constant was they always came through lawyers, always with confidentiality requirements, and always refused.

When I inherited the building two years ago, after first my mom, then my dad, passed away, the offers intensified. Not just every few years now, but every few months.

The latest had come just three months ago, when I'd applied for the planning permission. Whoever was behind these offers had been watching, waiting, keeping track of any projects involving the warehouse.

The question was why.

I ran my hand along the stone blocks the way Malakai had earlier when I was spying on the Lucky Break team through the window. Whatever secrets this place held, I wasn't giving up on it.

This down-on-its-luck warehouse was my chance to create something meaningful, to honor my family's history while building something new. And if that meant dealing with mysterious buyers and corrupt planning officials, so be it.

. . .

A week later, and I was no further ahead with the project other than the Lucky Break team having cleared the debris that had accumulated down the years. A week spent drooling over the enigmatic Malakai, enjoying the way his black Lucky Break Construction t-shirt rode up whenever he stretched.

Such was my obsession that I was as giddy as a teenager whenever he was near, something that happened with suspicious regularity. This had led to much internal admonishment as I did my best to wrangle my libido under control. I'd be the first to admit I was failing.

My other failure was in receiving the permits necessary for the project to move forward. The planning department had been rebuffing my lawyer and short of bribing people, I wasn't sure how to get the project back on track.

Once again up on the top floor in what had been Jeremiah's office, I took in the view of Coogan's Break and the California coast. Lost in the majesty of the setting sun, it took me a second to acknowledge my phone had buzzed.

However, when I collected it from the top of the old plan drawers, which were all that remained of Jeremiah's office, I came back to earth with a bump. It was an email from my assistant, telling me three clients wanted to make meetings for next week, two permit applications needed my review, and a reminder about the design presentation for the Millfield project.

On scrolling through the email a second time, I was conscious of the weight of my regular life trying to pull me back. I had a successful architectural practice in Redding, with projects that were progressing without fault under my senior associates' supervision. I didn't need to be in Coogan's Break, wrestling with a historic building and whatever complications came with it.

But I wanted to be here. For the first time in years, I was excited about a project in a way that went beyond professional satisfaction. This building spoke to me in ways my corporate commissions never had.

Maybe it was the family connection, or the challenge of preserving something with this much history. No matter the reason, I wasn't walking away without a fight.

Even if it meant spending more time around men like Malakai Torres.

I was still thinking about him twenty minutes later when I locked up the warehouse and headed to my Airbnb. The man watched everything with an intensity that should have made me uncomfortable.

Instead, I'd had to resist his animal magnetism whenever he was near. The way he moved with predatory grace, the way his eyes seemed to catalog every detail, and my visceral reaction when I caught his scent.

Something clean and masculine with an edge of danger that made my pulse quicken. Leaving me fighting the urge to lean into him, to see if he felt as solid as he looked.

What was wrong with me?

I'd always been attracted to safe men. Accountants, fellow architects, the guys who drove sensible cars and had retirement plans. Malakai Torres looked like the type who rode a motorcycle without a helmet and considered "retirement planning" to be making sure his emergency cash was hidden somewhere accessible.

And yet, every time those dark eyes met mine, I felt a jolt of pure attraction that left me reeling.

Nor had it lessened as the week progressed, with today being no exception. A day that had seen me double-checking measurements, hoping to head off any challenges from the planning department. Another day spent ignoring how Malakai quickened my blood and other body parts.

On reaching my rental, a cute Victorian cottage two blocks from the main drag, I'd convinced myself that my attraction to him was one-sided and born of frustration at my lack of progress with the project.

The cottage was what I needed after a day of wrestling with dust, paperwork, and hormones.

Hardwood floors, vintage fixtures, and a kitchen that looked like it had stepped out of a home decorating magazine. A place that made you want to bake cookies and host dinner parties.

I was dropping my laptop bag on the small chair next to the front door when my phone rang. The caller ID showed my lawyer's office in Redding.

"Hi, Norman."

"Amelia, I hope I'm not catching you at a bad time."

Norman Reyes had been handling my legal work for three years, ever since I went out on my own. He was thorough, honest, and had never called me after hours unless something was urgent.

"What's up?" I asked, expecting to hear of yet more hoops the planning department wanted me to jump through.

"I just got another offer for the warehouse. Same lawyer as before, but this time they're offering a lot more money."

There was something in his voice that had me moving my laptop bag to the floor so I could sit down on the hard-backed chair. "How much more?"

"Double the previous offer. They want to close within thirty days, cash deal, no inspections."

The number he quoted had my breath catching. It was more than enough to pay off my business loan, renovate my condo, and fund my practice's expansion.

Crazy money of the sort that would change everything.

"It's a generous offer," said Norman. "But the urgency strikes me as odd. Real estate deals involving historic buildings don't often come with this much pressure."

"Did they say why they wanted to close in such a rush?"

"Investment opportunity, according to their lawyer. They have plans for the property but need to move fast due to financing timelines."

I stared out the cottage window at the coast live oaks that lined the street. Three weeks ago, I'd arrived in town excited about the warehouse renovation. Now aware that someone was trying to sabotage the project, I was having second thoughts.

"Amelia? You still there?"

"I'm here. And I'm not interested."

"Are you sure? This is a lot of money."

"Norman, I'm sure."

But after I hung up, I wasn't sure about anything. The offer was tempting, more tempting than I wanted to admit. I could have taken the money, walked away from Coogan's Break and whatever complications the warehouse represented, and gone back to my orderly life in Redding.

Except I didn't want my boring life anymore. I

wanted this challenge, this building, this chance to create something meaningful.

And if I were being honest, I wanted to see more of Malakai Torres.

Which brought me back to the question of what was wrong with me.

I was still wrestling with that and the crazy money offer when there was a knock at the cottage door. After turning on the porch light, I stared through the peephole, surprised to see Malakai himself standing there, hands shoved in his pockets and an expression I couldn't quite read.

My heart did something stupid and fluttery as I opened the door.

"Sorry to bother you," he said. "I wanted to follow up on what happened last week with that guy from the city."

"Pruitt? The guy from the planning department?"

"He's legit," said Malakai, with me not missing the disappointment in his voice. "At least that's what it looks like. Works for the city, and has access to permit applications. But he's not supposed to be making house calls or discussing cost estimates. That's not his department."

I stepped aside to let him in, although he didn't do so until he'd kicked his work boots off and lined them up on the small front porch. Then there was no avoiding how he filled the doorway or how the cottage felt smaller with him in it.

"So, what you're saying is that the weedy little man was freelancing?"

"Or following orders from someone outside the planning department." Malakai's eyes scanned the cottage's main room, and I realized he was doing the same security assessment he'd done at the warehouse. "Nice place."

"It's temporary. If everything goes forward as I hope, I'm planning to live in one of the loft apartments once the renovation's done." I'd no sooner finished saying this than I realized it was true. Which was strange, given I hadn't even considered it until thirty seconds ago.

"About that." He turned those dark eyes on me, and I felt the same jolt of attraction. "I think you should be careful. Someone's going to a lot of trouble to discourage this project."

"You're not wrong. I just got another offer on the building," I paused before adding. "Double the previous amount."

His jaw tightened. "When?"

"Not ten minutes ago. They want to close in thirty days. An investment opportunity, apparently."

"You turned it down."

It wasn't a question, but I nodded anyway. "I'm not selling."

Something shifted in his expression, approval mixed with something that might have been relief. "That's good."

It was only when I realized I could see the gold flecks in his eyes that I became conscious of having moved closer to him. Close enough to catch the scent that had made me dizzy on many an occasion during the week.

And it wasn't just the cottage living room that felt charged with electricity. I was conscious of everything, my body zinging with a longing that had me wanting to move closer still.

The way his t-shirt stretched across his chest, the strength in his hands, the intensity of his focus when he looked at me. It was a powerful combination and one that had me forcing my hands down to my sides, if only to wipe my clammy palms on my jeans.

"Amelia." My name sounded different when he said it, rougher somehow.

"Yeah?" I said, my gaze locked with his.

"This might be a bad idea."

"What is?" I said, my words breathy.

Instead of answering, he cupped my face in his hands. His rough palms warmed me when I leaned into his touch without conscious thought.

"This," he said, and then his mouth was on mine.

The kiss was nothing like the careful, polite kisses I was used to. This was pure fire, demanding and hungry in a way that made my knees weak. His hands slid into my hair, and I pressed closer, wanting more of whatever this was between us.

When we broke apart, we were both breathing hard.

"That was a bad idea," I managed.

"The worst," he agreed, but he didn't step away.

"This isn't me. I don't do this," I said, as much to convince myself as him.

"Do what?"

"Kiss men I've only just met. Make impulsive decisions. Any of this."

His thumb stroked along my cheekbone. "What's your usual M.O.?"

"Plan everything. Think things through. Make sensible choices."

"And how's that working for you?"

I considered this, thinking about my ordered life, my successful but predictable career, and the safe relationships that never quite satisfied me.

"Not as well as I thought."

This time when he kissed me, I was ready for the fire and gave as good as I got, allowing myself to feel everything I'd been holding back. His hands roamed my back, pulling me closer, and I could feel his solid strength against me.

When his lips trailed down my throat, I made a sound that was part sigh, part moan. Everything about this was crazy, impulsive, and unlike anything I had ever done.

And I didn't want it to stop.

"Amelia," he said against my neck, his voice rough with want.

"Don't stop," I whispered, surprising myself with my boldness.

But he stopped, pulling back to look at me with an expression that was equal parts desire and regret.

"I should go."

"Should and want are two different things."

"Yeah, they are." His hands were still in my hair, and I could feel the tension in him, the battle between what he thought he should do and what he wanted to do. "I'm not in a position to offer you anything serious."

"Did I ask for serious?" I said, surprising myself. Who was I, and what had I done with Amelia Donovan?

Something flashed in his eyes at my wanton response, something hot and hungry that made my stomach clench with want.

"You're not the casual type."

"How do you know what type I am?"

"Because you're the sort of woman who renovates historic buildings and stands up to corrupt officials. You're the kind who makes plans and sees them through." His thumb traced my lower lip, and I had to fight not to take his finger into my mouth and suck on it, hard.

As if sensing this, he dropped his hand to my shoulder. "You're not the sort of woman who settles for less than she deserves."

"And what if what I want is standing right in front of me?"

My words surprised me as much as they seemed to surprise him. But they felt true in a way that made my chest tight. Not love. No, I wasn't naïve enough to call this love yet. But it was something real. Something worth exploring.

"Amelia." His voice was rough, and even more telling, it was uncertain.

"I'm not asking for forever," I said, reaching up to place my hand on his chest. "I'm just asking for right now. For the chance to see what this could be."

When had I become this bold? When had I started saying what I was thinking?

But I knew exactly when it had started. The moment I'd decided to renovate the warehouse instead of taking the safe route and selling it. Every choice since then had been a step away from the cautious woman I'd been and toward someone I was still discovering.

This new version of me didn't overthink every decision to death. She acted on instinct, trusted her desires, took risks that the old me would have run from. She was frightening and exhilarating, but she was exactly who I was.

I wasn't becoming someone different. I was becoming someone true.

Maybe it was this town, this warehouse, this whole crazy situation that had brought out a side of me I didn't know existed.

Or maybe it was him.

"You don't know what you're asking for," he said, but I could hear the resistance weakening in his voice.

"Then show me."

That was all it took. His mouth crashed down on mine again, and this time there was no hesitation, no holding back. His hands were everywhere, and I arched into him, wanting more, wanting everything.

When he lifted me onto the cottage's scrubbed pine kitchen table, I should have protested. Instead, I wrapped my legs around his waist and pulled him closer.

"Are you sure about this?" he asked, his voice rough with desire.

"I've never been surer of anything."

And in that moment, with his hands on my skin and fire racing through my veins, it was absolute.

For once in my life, I wasn't thinking about consequences or planning for tomorrow. I was living in that moment, in that feeling, in the connection that had sparked between us the instant we laid eyes on each other.

Whatever complications this brought, whatever trouble it caused, I'd deal with it later.

Right then, all I wanted was him.

THREE

MALAKAI

I should have walked away. Hell, I should have run.

But with Amelia's legs wrapped tight around my waist and her fists clutching my shirt like she'd never let me go, running was the last thing on my mind.

She tasted like coffee and sugar cookies, something sweet and addictive, something I wanted to drown in.

"You're sure about this?" I asked against her lips, giving her one last chance to stop me before I lost all control.

"Stop asking," she whispered, her voice husky with lust, "and start showing."

Christ. The prim architect, the woman who measured twice before she cut once, was gone. In her place was a wild, reckless stranger who wanted me inside her, now.

And I wasn't stupid enough to argue.

I dragged her shirt off, tossed it aside without a glance. The plain cotton of her sports bra hugged her curves, and somehow it was sexier than lace. Practical and unpretentious, but stretched tight across her breasts, her nipples already straining against the fabric.

"Beautiful," I muttered, my voice rough, my hands skimming her shoulders, down her arms, then back up to cup the soft weight of her breasts. She arched when I brushed my thumbs over her nipples, her moan vibrating straight down to my cock.

"Malakai..." The way she said my name, breathless and needy, undid me. I wanted her screaming it.

I kissed her throat, tasting sweat, dust, and something floral that clung to her skin. Her hands shoved at my shirt until I helped her rip it over my head. Her palms flattened against my chest, fingers trailing over muscle, tracing the scars carved into me. When she paused on one near my shoulder, curiosity softened her touch.

"What's this from?"

As Amelia traced the scar on my shoulder, I flinched.

"What's wrong?" She asked softly, her touch calming me.

"Nothing. Just... sometimes I forget that touch doesn't always mean danger." I caught her hand and brought it to my lips. "I'm working on it."

"How long has it been since someone touched you like this?"

The question hit me like a physical blow.

"Three years, two months—" I stopped myself. "A long time."

Her hand drifted lower, fumbling with my belt, but I caught her wrists. "Slow down, gorgeous. We've got time."

"I don't want slow," she shot back, eyes blazing with hunger. "I want you. Now!"

The command in her voice made my cock throb. This woman was full of surprises, and every one of them made me burn hotter.

I unbuttoned her jeans and shoved them down. She lifted her hips to help, leaving her in white cotton panties that left nothing to my imagination. And believe me, I had plenty. With her soft curves and flushed skin, she looked like every goddamn fantasy I'd ever had.

"Your turn," she murmured, tugging at my belt again. This time, I let her. She got my jeans open with impatient fingers, and I helped shove them down. Standing there in just boxers, my cock straining against the fabric, I caught the flicker of awe in her eyes before she touched me.

"I can't believe I'm doing this," she breathed, more to herself than me.

"Having second thoughts?"

Her gaze snapped up, steady. "No. First thoughts. The first real ones in a long time."

That hit something deep. But I didn't give her time to rethink. Instead, I unclasped her bra and let it fall. Her breasts spilled free, perfect handfuls, nipples tight and begging for my mouth. I bent and took one between my lips, sucking, teasing, making her cry out and clutch at my hair.

"Please..." she whispered, rocking against me.

I slid my hand down, under her panties. She was soaked. Her folds slick, her pearl swollen and waiting. I stroked it, teasing, and she writhed against my hand, biting back a moan.

"So wet for me," I growled against her breast. "So fucking perfect."

"Malakai," she gasped, shuddering. "I need—"

"I know," I cut her off, hooking my fingers in her panties and dragging them out of the way. She shuffled to the edge of the table, spreading her thighs wide, giving herself to me.

When she reached for my boxers, I let her push them down. My cock sprang free, thick and aching, and her hand wrapped around me. I groaned, bracing myself against the table as she stroked me with unsteady fingers.

"God, Amelia."

"I want you inside me," she begged, her eyes dark with raw need. "Please."

I should have asked about protection, but she was already pulling me in.

"I'm clean," I rasped.

"On birth control," she stuttered, with that all the permission I needed.

I positioned myself at her entrance, her slick folds parting around the blunt head of my cock. Her breath hitched as I pushed in, inch by inch, stretching her tight heat around me.

"Okay?" I asked, giving her time to adjust.

Her eyes fluttered closed, her body clenching around me like a fist. "More than okay," she whispered.

I started slow, savoring her heat, but she wasn't having it. Her nails dug into my shoulders as she urged me faster, harder.

"Don't hold back," she panted, before leaning back and hooking her ankles over my shoulders. "I won't break."

That broke my last shred of control. I drove into her hard and deep, with the table bucking under us. She met me thrust for thrust, her body rising to meet mine, her breasts bouncing with every movement. Her soft moans turned louder, wilder, until she was crying out my name.

"So good," she gasped, trembling. "So fucking good."

I reached down, thumb circling her pearl as I pounded into her. Her body jerked, back arching as she came, clenching tight around my cock. The sight of her unraveling, of her body gripping me so hard it was almost unbearable, shoved me over the edge.

I buried myself deep as I came, spilling inside her with a groan, my body shuddering against hers.

We stayed locked together, panting, trembling, neither of us willing to let go.

"That was..." she managed, voice hoarse.

"Incredible," I finished, still pulsing inside her.

She laughed, breathless, giddy. "I was going to say crazy."

I kissed her swollen lips, still tasting of coffee and sin. "Crazy works too."

And, fuck if I wasn't already hungry for more. "No regrets?" I asked.

"None," she said, not wasting time on niceties. "You?"

I should have had regrets. I should have thought about all the reasons this was a bad idea, all the ways this could go wrong. Instead, all I could think about was how right it had felt, how perfectly she fit in my arms, and how tightly she gloved my cock.

"None," I echoed.

She smiled, and it was like the sun coming out. "Good."

After pulling free and using a kitchen towel to clean her up, I helped her down from the table, both of us unsteady on our feet. She gathered her clothes, shy now that the moment had passed.

"You should—"

"Stay," I finished, surprising myself.

She looked up at me, and I could see the internal debate playing out in her eyes. But it wasn't really a debate anymore. The sensible part of her was losing ground to the woman hidden just under the surface.

That woman wanted me to stay.

"Okay," she said after a long pause. "But I should warn you, I don't do sleepovers either."

"I'm honored to be your first," I said, with her responding blush making her even more beautiful in my eyes.

We moved to the bedroom, and she disappeared into the bathroom while I pulled on my boxers and lay back on the bed. When she returned, she was wearing an oversized t-shirt that hit her mid-thigh and made her look younger, more vulnerable.

"Come here," I said, holding out my arm.

She climbed onto the bed, curling up next to me like she belonged there. And maybe she did. Maybe this crazy instant connection meant something more than just great sex.

"Tell me about the warehouse," I said, running my fingers through her hair. "What made you decide to renovate it now?"

She was quiet for a moment, thinking. "I've been successful in my career, but I haven't been happy. Everything felt so predictable, so safe." She paused, her fingers tracing idle patterns on my chest. "I kept designing buildings for other people's dreams while mine just... withered."

"What dreams?"

"Creating something that matters. Something with history, with soul." Her voice grew softer. "My great-great-grandfather built that warehouse with his sweat and blood. When I walk through those rooms, I can almost feel his determination, his hope. I want to honor that."

The passion in her voice made something shift in my chest. "And the offers to buy it?"

"Started small and got more persistent. But tonight's offer was different. More aggressive." She lifted her head to look at me. "What scares me is that I almost considered it. Not because of the money, but because... what if I'm not strong enough to see it through?"

"Hey." I tilted her chin, forcing her to meet my eyes. "You're the strongest person I've met. You took one look at that wreck of a building and saw possibility. That takes guts."

"Or stupidity."

"Courage," I corrected. "Trust me, I know the difference."

She studied my face in the dim light. "Is that why you left your old life? It took more courage than you had?"

The question hit closer to home than I'd expected. "Maybe. Or maybe I finally realized that surviving isn't the same as living." I traced her jawline with my thumb. "Being with you tonight... it's the first time in three years I've felt alive."

Her breath caught. "Malakai..."

"I know it's crazy. We don't know each other well. But when I look at you, I see someone who understands what it means to want more than just getting by."

"Two people with baggage finding each other," she whispered, echoing her earlier words.

"Maybe that's just what we need," I said, pulling her closer. "Someone who gets that the past doesn't have to define the future."

I wanted to tell her it was more than that, that she'd already gotten under my skin in ways I didn't think were possible. But it was too soon, too fast, even for someone who'd just had sex with a virtual stranger.

Instead, I held her closer, breathing in her scent and trying not to think about all the ways this could end, with none of them ideal.

For the first time in years, I wanted something more than just survival. I wanted a future, a real life, a chance to be the man she deserved.

The question I was facing now was whether my past would let me have it.

FOUR

AMELIA

I woke to the unfamiliar sensation of a warm, solid body pressed against my back and muscular arms wrapped tight around me. For a moment, I was disoriented.

Then the events of last night came flooding back, and I was hit with a wave of emotions that I couldn't quite name.

I'd slept with Malakai. After knowing him for not much more than a week.

I should have been horrified by my behavior. I should have been cataloging all the reasons this was a terrible idea and planning how to extract myself from this situation with whatever dignity I had left.

Instead, I was lying there thinking about how

perfectly I fit against him, how right it felt to wake up in his arms.

What was wrong with me?

His breathing was still deep, so I took my time turning in his arms in order to study his face. Asleep, he looked younger, less guarded. The lines around his eyes had smoothed out, and there was something almost vulnerable about the way his dark hair fell across his forehead.

Even relaxed, there was an edge to him. I could see it in the way he held himself, the subtle tension that never quite left his body. Whatever had happened in his past, whatever had sent him running for a fresh start, it had left marks.

The smart thing would have been to slip out of bed, make coffee, and have a rational conversation about how this had been nice but shouldn't happen again. We were going to be working together on the warehouse renovation, after all. Getting involved on a personal level would only complicate things.

But as I lay there watching him sleep, rational was the last thing I was feeling. I wasn't sure what I was feeling other than an overwhelming longing to have him bury himself in me over and over, my breath catching at the thought.

His eyes flashed open, alert in a way that spoke of years of training. For just a moment, I caught a glimpse of something dangerous in those dark depths before recognition set in and his expression softened.

"Morning," he said, his voice rough with sleep.

"Morning," I responded, conscious I was wearing nothing but an oversized t-shirt, that my hair was a disaster, and that I had morning breath.

"Sleep okay?"

"Better than I have in months," I admitted, and it was true. Despite the strangeness of the situation, I'd slept like the dead.

He smiled at that, and my heart did that fluttery thing again. "Good."

We lay there for a moment in comfortable silence, and I traced patterns on his chest without conscious thought. His skin, solid under my fingertips and scattered with scars, told of stories I knew I'd never hear.

"We should get up," I said, not making any move to do so.

"We should," he agreed, although his arms tightened around me. "The Lucky Break crew will be at the warehouse in a couple of hours," he added, still without moving.

"Hmmmm." My mumbled response both acknowledged his statement and confirmed for me how delicious I found the man next to me.

"I need to shower, get changed, and grab some

breakfast," he said, although he stayed right where he was.

"That sounds sensible," I said, feeling anything but.

Neither of us moved.

"This is crazy," I whispered.

"Which part?"

"All of it. Last night, this morning, the way I feel about you when I've yet to get to know you."

He was quiet for a moment, considering. "And what do you feel, Amelia?"

The question caught me off guard. What did I feel? Attraction, obviously. But it was more than that. There was something about him that made me want to throw caution to the wind, to take risks I'd never taken before.

"Like I'm not myself anymore," I said. "Like I'm someone braver, bolder. Someone who does things like this."

"Maybe you've always been someone like that. Maybe you just never had the right reason before."

The words hung between us, heavy with implication. Was he saying he could be the reason? Or was I reading more into this than he intended?

Before I could figure out how to respond, my phone buzzed on the nightstand. Rather than ignore the text, habit had me grabbing my phone and squinting at the screen in the morning light.

It was a text from my assistant. The permits for the warehouse renovation had been denied. All of them. All work on site was to stop.

"No," I gasped, sitting up, without a care that this had the sheet pooling around my hips.

"What is it?"

I handed him the phone, watching his expression darken as he read the message. Meanwhile, I was already out of bed, grabbing clothes from my suitcase. "I need to get to the planning office."

"I'll come with you."

"You don't have to do that."

However, he was already pulling on his jeans. "Yeah, I do."

Half-an-hour later, we were standing in the Coogan's Break planning office, facing a harried-looking clerk who seemed confused by the denial notices.

"I don't understand," she said, flipping through a file. "These permits were approved last week. I processed them myself."

She was still flipping through her paperwork when the glass door to the staircase opened with enough force that it slammed against the doorstop with an alarming rattle.

I turned to see an elegant woman in her seventies

entering the office, dressed in a navy suit, with silver hair like something out of a Wella advertisement. She moved with assurance, her mien that of someone who owned the room.

"Oh. Mrs. Quinn is here for her appointment," said the clerk.

I didn't catch what else she said under her breath, but her top lip curling told me it hadn't been complimentary.

My blood went cold. Something about the older lady seemed familiar, but I couldn't place her.

"You know her?" Malakai murmured, his lips close to my ear.

"I'm not sure," I said, my voice as hushed. "There's something about her..."

The Quinn woman's eyes swept the reception area, although she missed us on the first pass. But then she moved closer, squinting at me myopically, although even then she had trouble focusing on me, perhaps thanks to what looked to be the start of cataracts. For a moment, something predatory flashed across her features before she composed herself into a polite smile.

"Miss Donovan," she said, approaching with measured steps. "How nice to meet you in person. I heard you were in town working on the old warehouse."

"Mrs. Quinn?" I kept my voice neutral.

"Please call me Margaret. We townspeople are like family, after all." Her smile was razor-sharp and came nowhere near her eyes.

Malakai stepped closer to me, and Margaret's gaze flicked to him with calculating interest.

"And you?"

"Malakai Torres. I'm working on renovating the warehouse with Miss Donovan."

"How nice," said Margaret, her tone dismissive. Her attention then returned to me. "I hope you're not having any... difficulties with the project. These old buildings can be so challenging. Sometimes it's better to let sleeping dogs lie."

The threat was subtle but unmistakable.

I'd had no opportunity to ask her to explain herself when a brow-beaten woman shot out of an opening off to one side of the counter. "Mrs. Quinn, if you'll just come this way."

After watching the woman shown through to some inner sanctum, my gaze returned to the clerk, interested to see she'd also watched Margaret Quinn's departure.

With that done, she once again concentrated on the application forms in her folder. "Now, where was I?"

"You were looking to see why the approvals had

been reversed," I prompted, fighting to keep my frustration in check. "I received no approvals. Just the denial notices this morning."

"That's... that's not right." She looked up at us with worried eyes. "Someone would have had to override my approval. Only someone from the mayor's office could allow that." There was no mistaking that she'd then glanced over her shoulder at the doorway Margaret Quinn had just disappeared through.

Next to me, Malakai leaned forward, his presence somehow more intimidating despite his casual clothes and calm manner. "Are you saying the mayor reversed your decision?" Even if I hadn't been looking at him, I'd have been able to tell he was as gobsmacked by this as I was.

"Not necessarily," said the clerk. "Just give me a second."

Malakai and I waited while she hammered away on the keyboard in front of her, locating what it was she was after. Then, after checking over her shoulder, she spun the screen around so we could read it.

"Howard Pruitt," said Malakai, and my stomach dropped.

"The same Howard Pruitt who visited the job site not so long ago?" I said, my gaze locked on the poor clerk. "The same man who said nothing about the permits having been approved, and who then reversed them? That Howard Pruitt."

Her responding nod was tentative, with her perhaps sensing I was about to blow. She then turned the screen back around and typed some more. This time she leaned over the counter so she could keep her voice down. "It says here that there were issues with your application. Something about additional environmental impact studies being required."

I glanced at Malakai, who'd gone still beside me. "What environmental impact studies?"

"I'm not sure. Mr. Pruitt didn't fill in that section. Just made a note that the denials needed to go out ASAP." She looked between us with her face a study of nerves. "Is that a problem?"

"Yeah, I'd say that's a problem," said Malakai, his voice calm but with an edge that had the clerk taking a step back. "Can you tell us where we might find Mr. Pruitt today?"

"He's... he's marked as being away sick," she said, and if I hadn't been looking at her, I'd have missed her eyes widening with surprise.

We left the planning office with copies of the denial notices and a promise from the clerk to look into the situation. But I wasn't holding my breath for a quick resolution.

"This is harassment," I said as we walked back to Malakai's truck. "Pure and simple."

"Yeah, it is." He held the passenger door open for me, another gesture that shouldn't have made me feel as cared for as it did. "And Amelia, that Quinn woman? Yeah, she was Pruitt's passenger yesterday, the one manning the car horn."

By the time he'd walked around to his side of the car and gotten in, I was clenching my teeth so hard I was in danger of needing a crown. "Damn it. She has to be behind this. She just has to."

"The thing I want to know is why, and what we can do about it?"

"I'll call Norman, my lawyer, file an appeal, and fight this through proper channels."

"That could take months."

He was right, and we both knew it. That old lady, if it was her behind this, had played her hand with intelligence. She could tie up the permits forever, forcing delays that would cost me money I didn't have and derail the entire project.

Ten-minutes later, we pulled up in front of the warehouse to find the rest of the Lucky Break crew already there, standing around looking frustrated. Ethan approached as we got out of the truck.

"Let me guess," he said. "Permit problems?"

"Yes, but how did you know? Malakai and I have only just been to the city offices."

"Because someone called the building supply company this morning and canceled our material order. Said the project was on hold until further notice."

"What?!" The hits just kept coming. "Who called?" I knew full well it wouldn't have been anyone from my office.

"Someone claiming to represent you. They had your project number and knew all the details of our order." Ethan's expression was grim. "Whoever's doing this has access to information they shouldn't."

Daemon and Tyler joined us, both looking pissed off in equal measure. This was especially obvious on Daemon, who appeared to have had his nose busted in the past. Perhaps more than once.

Not that it looked bad on him. If anything, it added an edge that the women of Coogan's Break apparently found irresistible.

"We can reorder the materials," Daemon said. "But it'll push the start date back at least a week."

"That's if we get the permits sorted out," I said, nowhere near as confident as I had been.

I leaned against Malakai's truck, feeling overwhelmed. That morning I'd woken up feeling like I could take on the world. Now, it felt like the world was dismantling my project piece by piece.

"There's more," said Ethan, pulling out his phone. "I got a call from a historical society. Someone filed a complaint claiming the renovation plans don't meet preservation standards. They're threatening to file an injunction."

"That's impossible," I said. "I followed the planning department guidelines to the letter. I even exceeded their requirements in some areas."

"I believe you. But now we've got three separate agencies involved, all throwing up roadblocks at the same time." Ethan looked at Malakai. "This isn't coincidence."

"No, it's not," said Malakai, his expression tight. "And there's something else that doesn't add up. Amelia, that offer you got last night. They said it was an investment opportunity, right? Fast development timeline?"

"That's what Norman told me. Why?"

"Because if there's a historic preservation covenant on this building, no legitimate developer would touch it. Those covenants mean you can't demolish, can't make major structural changes without approval. It's a kiss of death for most commercial developments."

The pieces clicked together in my mind. "So, either the covenant is fake..."

"Or whoever's trying to buy the building has no intention of developing it," Malakai finished. "They want it for some other reason."

As the magnitude of what I was facing sank in, I could hear the Lucky Break team talking, but their voices seemed to come from far away. Whoever wanted this building had resources, connections, and the patience to wage a systematic campaign against me.

The anonymous offers, the inflated cost estimates, and now the coordinated assault on my permits and approvals. They weren't just trying to buy the building anymore. They were trying to force me into bankruptcy.

"Amelia." Malakai's voice cut through my spiraling thoughts. "Look at me."

I did, and the steady confidence in his eyes helped anchor me.

"We're going to figure this out," he said. "Whoever's doing this made a mistake by escalating this fast. Desperate people get sloppy."

"You think they're desperate?"

"I think something's changed. Maybe they found out you hired contractors; maybe they're working on their own timeline. Either way, they're pushing hard because they're afraid you'll succeed."

Ethan nodded. "He's right. If they thought you'd

give up, they wouldn't need to pull out all the stops like this."

"What am I supposed to do?" I said, looking at Ethan and then Malakai.

"We fight back," Malakai said. "But unlike them, we use our brains."

"How?"

"First, we document everything. Every call, every denial, every suspicious coincidence. Build a case for harassment." He paused. "Second, we figure out who's behind this, especially all those offers."

"I've been trying to do that for years," I said. "But they always come through lawyers and are always confidential."

"There are other ways to trace money," he said, and something in his tone suggested he knew what he was talking about. "People who know how to follow financial trails that others try to hide."

"That sounds expensive."

"Not as expensive as losing the building."

He was right. If I gave up, walked away from the warehouse and took whatever offer came next, I'd always wonder what would have happened if I'd fought back. And I'd have let whoever was doing this win.

"Okay," I said, straightening my shoulders. "What's the plan?"

Malakai smiled, and there was something predatory in the expression that should have worried me. Instead, it made me feel safer, knowing that particular look was directed at my enemies and not at me.

"The plan is we give them what they're not expecting," he said. "We stop playing defense and start playing offense."

Looking around at the Lucky Break crew, at these men who hadn't known me long but who would stand and fight for my project, I felt something shift inside me. The careful, cautious architect, who planned everything down to the last detail, was still there. But she'd been joined by someone fiercer, someone who wasn't willing to back down from a fight.

Someone who was worth knowing.

"Let's do it," I said.

And for the first time since this whole mess had started, I believed we could win.

The next evening, I found Malakai on my front porch, phone in his lap, a Bluetooth earpiece in one ear. He held up a finger when he saw me, finishing what sounded like a conversation about security protocols.

"Sorry," he said, pulling out the earpiece and

standing to join me. "Conference call with a client I couldn't avoid. Some are more persistent than others."

"You work late," I said, stepping aside so he could enter.

"Old habits," he said, walking inside. "How was your day with the lawyers?"

"Exhausting. But we're making progress." I studied his profile, unable to miss the tension in his jaw and the shadows under his eyes. "You look like you haven't slept.

"I sleep."

"When? You were here by six this morning, and you're still working now."

He was quiet for a long moment. "Sleep doesn't come like it used to. Too many balls in the air."

As if to reinforce this, his phone rang again, and he glanced at the caller ID and frowned.

"I need to take this," he said, stepping back out to the porch. Through the window, I watched him pace as he talked, his body language tense. When he came back inside, his expression was troubled.

"Bad news?" I asked.

"No. It could even be good news. But the timing's... interesting." He sat down with a thump. "That was someone I used to work with. There's been chatter about some kind of major federal operation in the works—DEA, FBI, the whole alphabet soup. Something big that's been building for years."

"Related to your... situation?"

"Maybe. It's hard to tell from the outside." He looked at me seriously. "Also, because of the way I've been investigating Margaret Quinn's background, I might have inadvertently sent up red flags with people I'd rather stay invisible to."

The admission seemed to surprise him as much as it did me. I reached over and took his hand, feeling the calluses, the barely healed cuts from construction work.

"What happened to you?" I asked softly.

"I told you—"

"Not the NDA version. The authentic version." I squeezed his hand. "Something broke you, Malakai. I can see it in the way you check exits when we enter rooms, how you never sit with your back to a door."

He stared out at the small garden in front of my Airbnb, jaw tight. "Trust got me betrayed. People I cared about paid the price."

"And now you don't trust anyone."

"I trust you." The words came out rough, like they'd torn something loose in his throat. "God help me, but I do. And that terrifies me."

My heart did something complicated in my chest. "Why?"

"Because caring about someone makes you vulnerable. Makes you weak."

"Or maybe it strengthens you." I turned in my chair to face him fully. "Maybe having something worth protecting gives you purpose."

He looked at me then, and I saw something raw and desperate in his eyes. "I can't lose anyone else, Amelia. I won't survive it."

"You won't lose me," I said, meaning it with everything I had. "We're building something here, remember? You and I, the team, the warehouse. We're creating something worth fighting for."

"I've had nothing worth fighting for in a long time."

"You do now."

He brought our joined hands to his lips, pressing a soft kiss to my knuckles. "When did you become so wise?"

"Someone taught me that courage isn't the absence of fear. It's doing what matters despite being afraid."

"Smart woman."

"She had an excellent teacher."

We sat in comfortable silence as darkness fell around us, still holding hands, both of us understanding that something had shifted between us. Something deeper than attraction, more solid than desire.

Something that felt dangerously close to forever.

FIVE

MALAKAI

On the drive back to Amelia's place, I couldn't shake the feeling we were being watched. The coordinated attack on the permits, the canceled materials, the historical society complaint, all of it smacked of a professional hatchet job.

Only after I'd gone through her cottage and checked every square inch for devices did I leave her to go through all the paperwork again. With her as safe as I could make her, I then drove straight to my place on the outskirts of town.

The house didn't look like much from the outside, but appearances could be deceiving. While most would take it as a ranch house sitting atop a concrete block walk-out basement, there was more to it than that. I'd spent the last three years making sure it was as secure as a fortress.

Motion sensors, cameras, reinforced doors, bulletproof glass. The neighbors thought I was paranoid. They didn't know how right they were.

Inside, I fired up my computer and started making calls. The first was to a contact in San Francisco who specialized in financial investigations. If someone were trying to buy the warehouse through shell companies and dummy corporations, Stefan would be able to trace the money.

"Malakai Torres," I said when he picked up. "I need a favor."

"Hell, Mal. I thought you were dead."

"I am," I said, unable to stop a snort of laughter. "That's why I need this to stay quiet."

There was a pause. "What do you need?"

I gave him the details about the warehouse offers, the lawyers involved, and the escalating pressure on Amelia. Stefan listened without interruption, although I could hear him making notes, his penmanship as heavy and scratchy as always.

"This'll take some time," he said after a while. "Financial trails through attorney trust accounts, they're hard to follow."

"How much time do you need?"

"Give me three or four days. I should have something for you by then."

My second call was to another old contact. This one was in government records. If Howard Pruitt was legitimate, there would be more on file than I'd uncovered with my rough-and-ready search. Employment records, background checks, performance reviews. Everyone left footprints, especially those involved in government at the state level.

"Carla, I need everything you can unearth about a city employee in Coogan's Break. Howard Pruitt, he works with the mayor."

"Piece of cake, sweet cheeks. Give me a couple of hours."

I was just hanging up when my motion sensors triggered. Someone was approaching the house. I checked the cameras and saw a familiar figure walking up my driveway.

Chase Hunter. Ethan's brother and a bail recovery agent.

I opened the door before he could knock. "If it isn't Chase Hunter, bounty hunter," I said, unable to resist ribbing him about his name-job connection. "What brings you by?"

"Ethan said I might be able to help you out with

something," he said, stepping inside without invitation. "My brother was vague about the details, so I thought I'd best hear it straight from the horse's mouth."

"Just helping a friend is all," I said, keeping my voice light.

Chase studied me with those sharp eyes that had made him one of the best bounty hunters in the area. "This friend of yours. She wouldn't be the architect working on that warehouse project, would she?"

There was no point in denying it. "Amelia's in trouble. Someone's targeting her project, trying to force her to sell."

"And you can help," said Chase, without so much as an ounce of doubt in his tone.

"I know I can. I just need to figure out who's behind it."

Chase moved to the window, scanning the street with the same automatic caution as I had earlier. "Ethan thinks someone's been conducting surveillance." After this small bombshell, he turned away from the window, as if to gauge my reaction. "But a smart boy like you, I guess you already knew that. What we need to know now is, are they watching you or are they watching her?"

"I'm not sure, although my gut tells me it's Amelia. But they made a mistake in escalating this fast. Desperate people get careless."

He nodded as if to himself before he spoke. "What do you need?"

His offer surprised me. I'd worked with Chase before on a few jobs that required both surveillance and tracking skills, but this was different. This was personal.

"I need to know if anyone asks questions about me. My background, my real identity, anything that might compromise my cover."

"I can do that. I'm on good terms with the guys down at the station. What else?"

"I want to set up cameras and motion sensors at the warehouse tomorrow night. See if anyone shows up after hours."

Chase nodded. "I can help you with that, too."

We spent the next couple of hours planning, even pulling out the schematics for the warehouse that Amelia had lent me. The biggest surprise was when Chase reached into the depths of his beat-up leather jacket and retrieved photocopied plans of the surrounding area. Even better was that the best vantage points for observation were already marked with a series of red circles.

It would appear my rusty climbing skills would be required after all.

The more hints I dropped about what had been going on, including the many offers to buy over the years, the quieter Chase got. And when he spoke, he kept his voice low. "This feels bigger than just someone wanting to buy a building," he said. "The level of coordination, the resources they're putting into this. It has to be more to it than a real estate deal."

"Yeah. And the question I keep asking myself is why they want it as much as they do, because I doubt it's to store stuff."

I'd just opened lite beers for myself and Chase when my phone buzzed with a text from Carla, my government contact. Howard Pruitt's background check was clean. Too clean. No disciplinary actions, no complaints, perfect performance reviews for the past five years. Either he was the most boring city employee in California, or someone had scrubbed his record.

"Anything useful?" Chase asked.

"Pruitt's background is squeaky. No one has a record that clean unless it's been scrubbed." And I knew how easy that was, having taken care of my own soon after I'd had that nasty boating 'accident'.

Chase tilted his head to the side as he thought about it. "Yeah, that or he's new to whatever game he's playing."

It was an interesting thought. Maybe Pruitt wasn't the mastermind. Maybe he was just another tool being used by whoever wanted the warehouse. This had me thinking about the mysterious Margaret Quinn, who'd popped up too often for it to be a coincidence. She didn't work for the city, which meant her involvement had to be personal.

With Chase heading out and us agreeing to meet tomorrow night, I had time for a quick shower before picking Amelia up for dinner. The Italian place on the waterfront had outdoor seating with views of the bay, and I'd snagged us a table for two.

She was waiting for me when I arrived at her cottage, wearing a simple dark purple dress that somehow managed to be both elegant and seductive as hell. Her hair was loose around her shoulders, and she'd put on just enough makeup to highlight those incredible dark eyes.

"You look beautiful," I said, meaning every word.

"Thank you." She smiled, and I felt a familiar kick to my chest. "You clean up pretty well yourself."

Dinner was perfect. Good food, decent wine, and conversation that flowed as easily as everything else between us. We talked about her architectural practice and my time with Lucky Break, both of us careful to avoid the current situation.

But underneath the casual conversation, there was an undercurrent of heat that was ever building. Every time she laughed, every time her fingers brushed mine reaching for her wineglass, every time she looked at me with those dark eyes, the tension ratcheted higher.

The drive back to her cottage felt electric, both of us well aware of the other's presence. When I walked her to the door, neither of us was pretending this was just a friendly dinner anymore.

"Would you like to come in?" She said, her eyes already saying yes to a lot more than coffee.

"I was hoping you'd ask," I said.

The moment we were through the door, we were all over each other, any thoughts of coffee long forgotten. She pressed me back against the small kitchen island, her mouth claiming mine with desperate hunger. All the careful control I'd maintained during dinner evaporated in an instant.

"I've been thinking about this all night," she gasped against my lips.

"All day," I corrected, my hands already working at the zipper of her dress.

"God, yes."

There was nothing slow or careful about this. We were tearing at each other's clothes, desperate to get closer, to feel skin against skin. Her dress hit the floor, followed by my shirt and pants.

"Bedroom," she managed between kisses, while I concentrated on removing her lacy bra and panties, being careful not to rip the sheer fabric.

"Too far," I growled before spinning her around and leaning her over the kitchen island, where I nudged her feet apart.

Not to be outdone, she spread herself even wider, jutting her sex in my direction in open invitation. Her "Malakai, I need you. Now!" was heavy with desire.

I didn't need to be told twice, and on slamming myself home, we both cried out at the intensity of it. This was pure need, desperate and all-consuming.

"Yes," she gasped, hanging onto the kitchen island as if her life depended on it. "Just like that."

I gave her everything I had, driving into her with an intensity that had my body screaming for release. She met me thrust for thrust, driving herself back against me in perfect harmony.

"So good," she panted. "You feel so good inside me."

I could feel her getting close, her body tensing around me. When she came, crying out my name, her core gripped me, pulling me over the edge. But I wasn't ready to let her go just yet, which saw us holding her tight for long moments, both of us breathing hard, our bodies still joined.

"We should move to the bedroom," she said.

"Can you walk?" I asked only half joking.

"I guess we'll find out."

We made it, but only just, falling onto her bed in a tangle of limbs. And then we started all over again, this time with the luxury of time and space to explore each other to our heart's content.

I learned she was ticklish behind her ears, that she made the most incredible sounds when I used my mouth on her breasts, that she wasn't shy about telling me what she wanted. And even better was her being open to experimenting.

She learned I lost all control when she took me in her mouth, with her wielding her power over me. Most explosive of all was that I could make her come just by sucking hard on her pearl while fingering her.

By the time we collapsed, exhausted and sated, the cottage's bedroom felt like our own private world.

"I should leave you to get some sleep," I said, though I made no move to leave.

"Don't you dare," she replied, curling up against my side. "I want you here all night."

"You sure about that?"

"Absolutely!" She lifted her head to look at me. "You'd best get some sleep, Mal, because I'll want you again in the morning!" Her filthy grin after this was enough to have me once again wide awake.

However, I knew she was right. We both needed sleep, with my holding her as she drifted off, marveling at how right this felt. At the start of the month, I was a man with no genuine connections, no one who mattered enough that I'd risk my new identity.

Now I had Amelia, and everything had changed.

Whatever tomorrow brought with my surveillance plans, whatever Chase and I discovered about who was targeting her, I knew one thing for certain.

For the first time in years, I wasn't just surviving. I was living.

The next afternoon, I was at the warehouse double-checking all our equipment when something out front of the building caught my attention. A dark sedan, the same one Pruitt had been driving when he visited the warehouse the week before. Ethan was right. It had to be decades old, but it gleamed like it had just rolled off a showroom floor.

Five minutes later it passed by again, and this time I was ready for it. However, in the exact second I took the photo, another car blocked my shot. Not wanting to be caught that way again, I made it down to the first floor in time to see the sedan passing yet again. This time I got a clean photo of the license plate.

Even better was that the car had been far enough along the road that when I zoomed in I was able to see the occupants, if only the backs of their heads. It was enough to confirm the passenger had to be Margaret Quinn, her silver hair a testament to this.

That the top of the driver's head only just cleared

the back of his seat told me it was likely that Pruitt guy. Did I think that was a coincidence?

Hell no, I didn't. For one thing, I didn't believe in those.

After making a note of the license plate, I called Chase.

"I need you to run a plate for me," I said when he answered.

"Shoot."

I gave him the number along with the make and model, and within minutes, he came back to me. "Registered to Richard Pearson, home address on Maple Street."

"Pearson... wait, that rings a bell. Amelia mentioned that a woman by that name had approached her aunt years ago about selling the warehouse."

"Want me to dig deeper into this Pearson connection?" Chase asked.

"No," I said. "Anyone targeting Amelia has to come through me first.

I woke to the sound of Amelia humming in the kitchen and the smell of quality coffee, not the cheap stuff I'd been living on. For a moment, I just lay there, listening to her move around, amazed by how right it felt to wake up in her space.

When I padded out to find her, she was standing at the stove in a t-shirt and nothing else, stirring something in a pan.

"Morning," I said, wrapping my arms around her from behind.

"Hmmm." She leaned back against me. "I hope you like scrambled eggs. It's about the only thing I can cook without burning down the house."

"I'll be happy with anything you make." I pressed a kiss to her neck, tasting sleep and contentment.

"Flatterer." But she was smiling. "Coffee's on the counter."

I reluctantly let her go and poured myself a mug, watching her work. She moved with the same careful precision she brought to everything. Measuring, timing, checking. It was soothing.

"You know," I said, "I can't remember the last time someone made me breakfast."

"Really?" She glanced over her shoulder, surprised.

"Really. Most of the time I'm as happy with protein bars and takeout."

"That's terrible." She turned off the burner and faced me. "No wonder you're so skinny."

I laughed. "Skinny?"

"Lean," she corrected, eyes twinkling. "Attractively lean."

"Better."

She divided the eggs between two plates, adding toast she'd apparently made while I was sleeping.

As we sat at the pine table, my mind's eye filled with the last thing I'd eaten off its scrubbed surface, and that had been Amelia, with her spread before me like the finest meal.

It took every ounce of my self-control to rid myself of that filthy image and instead concentrate on my current meal.

"This is nice," I said without thinking.

"What is?"

"This. Normal. Sitting here with you like we do this every morning."

She paused with her fork halfway to her mouth. "There's no reason we couldn't. You know, do this every morning."

The casual way she said it made my chest tight. "Amelia..."

"I'm not asking for promises," she rushed. "I just mean... I enjoy having you here. You make the space feel more like a home and less like an Airbnb."

"You make me feel less empty too," I rushed out.

The words surprised us both. She set down her fork, reaching across the table to cover my hand with hers.

"I know this is moving fast," she said. "I know we should slow down, be sensible."

"But?"

"But I don't want to be sensible. Not with you." She squeezed my hand. "For the first time in my life, I want to follow my instincts instead of my head."

"What are your instincts telling you?"

She was quiet for a long moment, studying our joined hands. "That you're it for me. Whatever this is, it's real. That I'd rather risk everything with you than play it safe alone."

I brought her hand to my lips, kissing her palm. "My instincts are saying the same thing."

"Good," she said, smiling. "Then we're both crazy together."

"The best kind of crazy."

Later that morning, as Amelia worked on yet more permit paperwork and I reviewed security plans, I kept catching her stealing glances at me. There was something domestic about the scene, with both of us working at her small table, the morning light streaming through the windows.

"You're staring," I said without looking up from my tablet.

"Just thinking."

"About?"

She set down her pen, considering her words.

"About how different this feels from other relationships I've had."

That got my attention. I looked up, waiting for her to continue.

"Usually, I overthink everything. Analyze compatibility, plan out potential futures." She gestured between us. "But with you, I'm just... here. Present. Not worried about what comes next."

"Is that good or bad?"

"Terrifying," she admitted. "But good. Like maybe I've been living life with the brake on, and you're teaching me what it feels like to let go a little."

I closed my tablet, giving her my full attention. The woman who'd been so careful, so controlled when I'd first met her, was sitting here admitting she was learning to take risks. Because of me.

"I've been nobody's teacher before."

"What have you been up to instead?"

"Careful. Closed off. The type of man who doesn't stick around long enough to teach or learn anything meaningful." My smile felt rueful. "You're changing that."

"Good," she said, and the certainty in her voice did something to my chest. "We're changing each other."

The simple truth of it hit me then. For three years, I'd been surviving. With Amelia, I was living again. More than that, she'd become essential. Not just someone I wanted, but someone I needed. Someone whose absence would leave me empty in ways I couldn't fix. The realization should have terrified me.

Instead, I felt complete in ways I hadn't in a long time.

SIX

AMELIA

I woke up alone, which should have disappointed me more than it did. But the note from Malakai, along with the lingering scent of his cologne on the sheets, had me smiling instead.

Had to leave early for work.
Last night was incredible.
See you later today. M

Phew, he wasn't wrong. The passion between us was unlike anything I'd ever experienced, and waking up in his arms just as dawn was breaking for another round of lovemaking had left me feeling both sated and wanting more.

After stretching like a cat and reveling in my body being sore in all the right places, I tried to summon some regret about last night. The old Amelia would have been spiraling by now, making lists of all the reasons this was a mistake, planning damage control strategies. But I felt... content. Alive in a way I hadn't experienced in years.

When had I become someone who sought safety over satisfaction? Somewhere along the way, when had responsible morphed into afraid. Afraid of wanting too much, risking too much, feeling too much.

But Malakai made me want to throw all of that careful control out the window. He made me want to take risks, to trust my body and my heart instead of my calculating mind. The realization should have terrified me. Instead, it felt like coming home.

But, much as I wanted to, I couldn't sleep the day away, with me grabbing my phone off the bedside table and opening up my emails.

The first had been sent the night before and was from Norman, my lawyer, saying he'd filed all the appeals but reiterating the process could take months. The second sent at an ungodly hour that very morning was from my assistant, reminding me about a conference call with the Millfield project clients at two.

I was speaking with her on voicemail when a text arrived from Mal.

> Hope you're caught up on your sleep, sweet thing, because I've picked up a few things we can try out later.

It took all my self-control not to giggle before I rushed to end the call. The office staff were already looking at me funny thanks to my obsession with the warehouse.

No need to confirm it by acting the fool within earshot of a staff member. And it wasn't just my mood that was buoyant, with my body thrumming in response to Malakai's filthy promise, as was doubtless his intention.

Well, two can play at that game, Mr. Torres. While I wouldn't usually put something this scandalous in type, Mal made me do things I'd never have dared to do in the past. Let's see how he got on spending the morning in a constant state of arousal.

I'd hit send and was laughing to myself when my phone rang. For a second I thought it was Malakai determined to take our e-flirting up a notch. But it was my lawyer, with my stomach dropping in response.

"Norman? Please tell me you have good news."

"Yes, I do. Your building permits were reinstated

five minutes ago. All of them. Someone higher up overruled Pruitt's decision."

"That's wonderful, but why the sudden change?"

"I'm not sure. The clerk I spoke to said new information had come up about the environmental impact requirements. Apparently, they don't apply to your project after all."

I should have been relieved, but something felt off about the timing. Yesterday we'd been under siege from multiple agencies, and now everything was resolved? Much as I wanted to believe it had all been a clerical error, I had my doubts.

"Norman, is it possible this is a trap? Make us think we're in the clear and then pull the permits again?"

"It's possible, but unlikely. The approvals came from the mayor's office. That's pretty high up the food chain for games."

After I hung up, I called Malakai, but it went straight to voicemail. This had me calling Ethan to let him know the good news, with him pleased to be able to get the project underway.

After a quick shower, I attempted to handle my remaining business calls, but it was hopeless. All I could do was think about Malakai's past and the pain I'd seen in his eyes when he'd talked about betrayal and loss. This proved there were layers to this man that had nothing to do with the attraction between us and everything to do with who he was when no one was watching.

By late morning, I missed him in a way that surprised me. Not just physically, though there was that too. I missed his presence, the way he made me feel simultaneously protected and challenged.

When he texted asking if I wanted company for dinner, I typed and deleted three different responses before settling on: *Yes. Always yes.*

His response was immediate: *Always?*

I stared at the word for a long moment. Was I ready for always? The old Amelia would have backtracked, made a joke, kept things light. But the woman I was becoming, the one who was renovating a falling-down warehouse instead of taking the safe path...

Soon enough, I typed *Always* in response, and meant it.

I was now less able to concentrate than before, and so after a late lunch, I drove to the warehouse to see what was happening.

The sight that greeted me there was encouraging. The Lucky Break crew was busy preparing for construction, with equipment being loaded in through the large rear doors. Ethan waved when he saw me, looking happier than he had since we'd started dealing with the permit problems.

"Great news about the approvals," he called out. "It won't take us long to catch up on lost time."

"Where's Malakai?" I asked, looking around.

"He left about an hour ago. Said he had some research he had to take care of, but that he'll be back here later."

"Did he say what time?"

"Around four or five, I think. He and Chase, my brother, had some equipment they needed to beef up security."

At my look of confusion at his brother helping Malakai, he'd added, "Chase is a bounty hunter. He's got contacts that will come in handy."

That made sense, I supposed. With construction beginning Monday, it would be important to make sure whoever had been messing with the project didn't escalate to damaging equipment or materials.

I spent another hour at the warehouse, reviewing the construction timeline with Ethan and making sure everything was ready for Monday. The permit approvals meant we could proceed as planned, which should have made me ecstatic.

And yet I couldn't shake the feeling that something was wrong. The sensation stayed with me as I hurried around the supermarket on my way home.

By five o'clock, I was back at my cottage, trying to focus on the paperwork I'd avoided that morning, with about as much success. I kept checking my phone, expecting to hear from Malakai, but there was nothing.

An hour later, I was chopping vegetables for a salad to go with the rotisserie chicken I'd picked up, when my phone rang.

"Hey, beautiful," Malakai's voice was like honey but distracted. "I'm really sorry, but something's come up, and so I won't be able to make it for dinner after all. I thought I'd better let you know before you went to any trouble."

"That's okay," I said, looking at the half-prepared salad and the wine glasses at the ready. "Does it have something to do with security?"

"Something like that. We want to make sure no one tries anything now that the hold on the permits has been lifted."

"Is that necessary?"

There was a pause. "Doubtless not, but the sooner we get everything installed, the better. I should be free by tomorrow morning."

"Will you come by for breakfast?"

"Try to stop me."

The warmth of his voice made me smile. "Malakai. Be careful tonight."

"Always am. Get some sleep, gorgeous. You'll need it for what I've got planned in the morning."

After we hung up, I felt better, if a little horny.

Whatever Malakai and Chase were doing, they were professionals. They could handle themselves.

After I'd had dinner and tidied everything away, I settled on the couch in the dark with my e-reader, trying to relax for the first time in days. The permits were approved, construction was starting Monday, and I had an incredible man in my life who made me feel things I'd never felt before.

I was so absorbed in my book that I almost missed the sound of a car stopping out front, but when I glanced out the window, I saw nothing unusual. I couldn't even see the flare of headlights and so put it down to a neighbor coming home from dinner.

But then I heard footsteps on the front path, and they didn't match Malakai's confident stride. Instead, these were the footsteps of someone trying to be quiet.

Stealthy enough that I slammed the cover shut on my e-reader, hoping to give my eyes time to adjust to the dark. There was nothing natural about my reaction, with this having more to do with the spy thriller I was reading than my usual behavior.

Only when I could no longer see the glare of the e-reader when I closed my eyes, did I move over to the front window and peer through the lace curtains. There was a figure in dark clothes moving around the side of the cottage, heading toward the back.

My heart hammered against my ribs, each beat

echoing in my ears. This wasn't Malakai or anyone else who should be here.

I grabbed my phone off the coffee table and dialed 911, but before I could hit send, I heard the unmistakable sound of the back door being forced open.

Someone was inside the cottage.

I looked at the front door, but whoever was making their way down the narrow hallway was fast approaching. There wasn't time to unlock it and get away clean. And even if I made it outside, where would I go then?

This saw me ducking into the bedroom and taking care to close the door without a sound. That done, I grabbed the first weapon I could find. In this case, the heavy ceramic lamp from the bedside table I was sure had come from Pottery Barn rather than the local antiques center.

Through the thin bedroom door, I could hear whoever it was moving through the cottage, opening drawers, rifling through papers. They were looking for something specific.

My laptop was in the living room, along with all my project files for the warehouse. If they were after information about the renovation, they'd find plenty.

But I wasn't going to just hide and hope they left.

These people had been harassing me for days, and I was done being a victim.

Loath as I was to lose my weapon, I put the lamp down before opening the bedroom window, thankful the cottage was only one story. Even better was that the window faced the side yard, away from where I'd seen the intruder approaching.

As quietly as I could, I climbed out the window and dropped to the ground. My bare feet hit the cold grass, and I realized I was still wearing just the t-shirt and yoga pants I'd put on after my shower.

But I was out, and I had my phone.

After re-closing the window as best I could, I crept around to the front of the cottage, where I hid behind my car while I dialed Malakai's number.

"Please pick up," I whispered as it rang.

"Amelia? What's wrong?"

"Someone's in my cottage," I whispered. "I heard them come in through the back door, and I know damned well it was locked. I'm hiding outside."

"Where are you?"

"Behind my car in the driveway."

"Good. Stay there. Do not go back inside. I'm on my way."

"Should I call the police?"

"I'll handle that. Just stay hidden and stay on the line with me."

Through the cottage windows, I could see lights moving around inside. Whoever was in there was being thorough, going through everything.

"They're still inside," I whispered to Malakai. "I can see flashlights."

"How many?"

"I'm not sure. I saw only one person outside, but there could be more."

"Okay. I'm only minutes away. Just stay put."

But even as he said it, I heard someone stumbling around down the side of the house.

"I think they're leaving," I whispered.

"Don't move. They might come around front."

He was right. A moment later, I heard footsteps on the gravel driveway, getting ever closer to where I was hiding. I pressed myself down behind the car, trying to make myself as small as possible.

The footsteps paused on the other side of my car, and I held my breath, afraid that even the sound of my breathing would give me away.

Then I heard a car door open and close, followed by an engine starting. Headlights swept across the cottage as whoever it was backed out of the driveway and drove away.

"They're gone," I whispered to Malakai.

"I'm almost there. Do not go inside until I get there."

"I won't."

But as I crouched there behind my car, looking at my violated cottage, I felt a surge of anger that surprised me with its intensity.

These people had been playing games with my permits, sabotaging my project, and now they'd broken into my home.

Whatever they were looking for, whatever they thought they'd accomplish, they'd just made this personal.

And I was done playing defense.

"Malakai?" I said into the phone.

"Yeah?"

"When you get here, we need to talk. I want to know everything you've found out about who's behind this."

"Amelia..."

"Everything," I repeated. "No more protecting me from the truth. If I'm going to fight back, I need to know what, or who, I'm fighting."

There was a pause, then: "Okay. But first, let's make sure you're safe."

As I waited for him to arrive, still crouched behind my car in the chilly night air, I made myself a promise.

Whoever was doing this to me had just made their biggest mistake.

They'd brought the fight to my home.

It was about time I returned the favor.

SEVEN

MALAKAI

I made it to Amelia's cottage in record time, abandoning my fruitless search for the owner of the sedan I'd seen Pruitt driving. The tip I'd uncovered late afternoon looked to have been a bust, with me now wondering if I hadn't been sent on a wild goose chase to keep me away from Amelia.

A second after my truck slid to a stop, I was out and scanning the area. The cottage was dark, with no signs of forced entry from the front that I could see.

My hand dropped of its own volition to my sidearm, muscle memory from years of approaching hostile locations taking over. My hand closing on thin air was jarring. Three years later, and I still reached for weapons that weren't there.

I forced my breathing to slow, my movements to appear casual. Civilian Mal Torres checking on his girlfriend, not Malcolm Tremaine conducting a tactical assessment. But my eyes still swept the area with military precision, cataloging sight lines, escape routes, potential concealment. Some training never left you.

"Amelia?" I called, careful to keep my voice low.

Her head popped up from behind her car, and the relief that flooded through me was staggering. She was okay. Everything else we could deal with. The terror I'd felt driving here, imagining her hurt or worse, had shown me something I'd been trying not to acknowledge. Something I couldn't afford to avoid any longer.

"Right here," she whispered.

I hurried to her side, pulling her into my arms and holding her tight. She was shaking, whether from cold or adrenaline I wasn't sure, but she felt real against me.

"You're okay," I said, more to convince myself than her.

"I'm fine. Just angry."

I could hear it in her voice, the steel beneath the fear. This woman was tougher than she looked and smarter than whoever had broken into her home.

The sight of Amelia's violated cottage triggered something cold in my chest. Upturned furniture, scattered papers visible through the windows. It was all too familiar. Too much like the aftermath of raids I'd conducted in another life.

For a moment, I was back in Syria, standing outside a house we'd just cleared, knowing innocent people had been terrorized in the name of gathering intelligence.

"Mal?" Amelia's voice pulled me back to the present, and I forced myself to focus on her face, not the crime scene behind her. "Sorry. I'm just surprised they'd risk breaking in when someone was home. Tell me what happened."

"They didn't realize I was there," said Amelia, her voice trembling. "I was on the couch reading my e-reader in the dark. It's easier for me to lose myself in the story that way."

She then walked me through it all. The car stopping outside, the figure moving around the cottage, the sound of the back door opening when she didn't even have a key. How she'd escaped through the bedroom window instead of panicking or trying to confront the intruder.

"Smart thinking with the window," I said, dropping a reassuring kiss on her forehead. "Many people would have frozen or tried to hide in place."

It was enough to have me holding her tighter, while pulling out my phone with my free hand and calling Chase. He answered on the first ring.

"Change of plans," I said. "Someone just broke into Amelia's place. I need you to come here first, and then we'll hit the warehouse."

"How long ago?"

"Maybe twenty minutes. They're gone now, but I want you to process the scene before we go inside."

"On my way," he said after I'd rattled off the address.

With help on the way, I ended the call and looked at Amelia, noticing for the first time that she was still in just a t-shirt and yoga pants. Even worse was that she was in bare feet.

"Let's get you into my truck where it's warm. Chase will be here in a few minutes, then we'll go inside and see what's up."

"Chase? I thought he was a bounty hunter."

"Yeah, he is, but he's also got experience when it comes to crime scenes. If there's evidence to find, he'll spot it." I fell silent for a moment before adding, "Plus, the cops know him."

There was no need for me to spell it out for her that my preference was to keep a low profile, with the look she gave me saying she understood.

We sat in my truck with the heater running, Amelia curled up next to me. I could feel the tension in her body, the way she kept glancing at her violated cottage.

"This is connected to the warehouse, isn't it?" she said. "The permits being approved and then this happening on the same day. It's not a coincidence."

"No, it's not."

"Someone's getting desperate," she said, snuggling even tighter against my side.

"That's my take on it, too. But what were they looking for?" The question I didn't voice was whether the intruder would still have broken in if they'd known she was there. Instinct told me the answer was yes.

Chase arrived in his pickup and parked across the street, where he dragged a small duffel bag of equipment out of the passenger side, his expression grim.

"I don't suppose you've called the cops," he said, raising an eyebrow for my benefit.

"No, I didn't think that was a good idea. Thought it was best to see what we're dealing with first."

Chase nodded. "Smart. Let me look before we contaminate the scene any more than necessary."

After getting Amelia to tiptoe inside and turn on all the lights to avoid any extra fingerprints, he spent twenty minutes going over the cottage inside and out. Only when that was complete, did he signal us over; his expression troubled.

"Professional job," he said. "They knew what they

were doing. The back door was picked, not forced. Minimal damage, precise work."

"So not random burglars," said Amelia after dragging on a sweatshirt.

"Not even close. If this were a burglary, they'd have taken the TV and anything else not nailed down." Chase looked at me. "But they wanted something, and they had the skills to get it without making a lot of noise."

Even so, the damage was worse than I'd expected. They'd been thorough. Every drawer in the kitchen had been opened and searched. The living room was a disaster, with the couch cushions pulled off, and papers scattered everywhere.

"They were looking for something specific," said Chase, taking yet more pictures of the chaos. "This wasn't a random search. Whoever they were, they had a plan."

In the bedroom, it was the same story. Dresser drawers pulled out, the closet ransacked, even the mattress had been pulled askew.

"My laptop!" said Amelia after closing the bedroom window. "Where's my laptop?!"

We found the bag on the living room floor with the laptop still inside, proving Chase's assertion that it wasn't a simple burglary. Even so, the intruder had still gone through the bag. According to Amelia, as well as the power cable, several USB drives that had been in the side pocket were also missing.

"They took the storage devices but left the computer," observed Chase. "That tells us something."

"What?" Amelia asked.

Worried about her reaction, I draped my arm across her shoulders before I answered her. "They wanted your files. But they didn't want you to know too soon what was missing. If they'd taken the laptop, you'd have known right away. This way, you might not notice the missing drives for days."

This, in concert with the professional nature of the break-in, was giving me a picture of what we were dealing with, and I didn't like it. "Amelia, what was on those drives?"

Her brow crinkled as she cast her mind back to what might be on them, although it soon cleared. "Backups of historic project files. Even some earlier drawings relating to the warehouse renovation." She paused, thinking. "And my research into the building's history. I've been digitizing old family documents, property records, anything I can find about the original construction."

"There's our motive," I said. "Someone wanted to know what you'd found out about the warehouse's past."

Chase, having photographed anything that moved,

and a fair amount that didn't, was busy packing up his equipment. "I've documented what I can, but without official status, I can't process this scene like the cops would. You two need to decide whether you're calling this in."

I looked at Amelia. "Your call. But if we involve the police, it becomes public record. Let's not forget the bastards behind this have already shown themselves to be capable of hacking into places they shouldn't."

She nodded in understanding. "And that'd mean they knew we'd reported the flash drives as stolen."

"That's the trade-off," said Chase. "Official investigation versus keeping our cards close to our chest," his response worded in such a way as to confirm he now considered himself a part of the team.

Amelia and I stood in the middle of her destroyed lounge, and as she took in the trashing of what had been her private space, I could see her anger building.

"Let's handle it ourselves for now," she said. "If these people want to play dirty, we'll play dirty right back."

Chase grinned. "I like her."

"Okay," I said, my arms wrapped tight around Amelia, "we'll play dirty, but because we're not involving the cops, you can't stay here tonight."

"I'll get a hotel room."

"No. You'll stay with me."

She protested, but I cut her off. "My place is secure in ways not even the best hotel in town is. Motion sensors, cameras, reinforced everything. If they want to get to you there, they'll have to go through a lot more than a picked lock."

"Mal, I can't just move in with you."

"Why not? We're sleeping together anyway, and right now you need protection more than you need independence."

Chase cleared his throat. "Much as I hate to interrupt this domestic discussion, we've got surveillance to set up at the warehouse. If these people are escalating, then we can't afford to muck about."

He was right. With Amelia's cottage ransacked and her research files stolen, whoever was behind this might think they had enough information to act.

"Go," said Amelia. "Do your surveillance thing. I'll pack a bag and meet you at your place later."

"No. I'm not leaving you alone."

"I'll be fine. I won't let them scare me into hiding."

I could see the stubborn set to her jaw, the same determination that had gotten her this far. But I also knew how dangerous desperate people could be.

"Compromise," I said. "Pack your bags, then come with me to the warehouse for the surveillance setup. After that, we head back to my place. You can leave your car here."

She considered this for a moment. "What about my work tomorrow? I've got calls scheduled."

"You can work from my place. I've got excellent internet and more security than the Pentagon."

"More security than the Pentagon?" said Chase, snorting. "That's a hell of a claim."

"A different type of security," I said. "The kind that keeps people out rather than information in."

While Amelia busied herself with packing a bag, Chase and I set about securing the back door so it would at least slow down any future attempts at entry. I also made a mental note to install better locks after this was over.

"She's tougher than she looks," murmured Chase while we worked.

"Yeah, she is."

"Good thing, considering what you might have gotten her into."

I paused in my work on the door frame. "What's that supposed to mean?"

"Come on, Mal. You think I don't recognize the signs?" said Chase before glancing at the bedroom door. Even with all the noise Amelia was making, it was still a relief when he dropped his voice even further before carrying on.

"Someone with your skill set, your background, doesn't end up working construction in a small town by accident. You're hiding from something, and now whatever that is might have found you."

"This isn't about me," I hissed. "This is about the warehouse."

"Maybe. Or maybe someone's using the warehouse to get to you. Which means they're using her." Chase straightened up, fixing me with that penetrating stare. "Either way, that woman is now in danger. What are you going to do about it?"

"Whatever it takes to keep her safe."

Chase again looked to the bedroom door before muttering, "Even if it means walking away?"

His question hit me like a punch to the gut. Walk away from Amelia?

"It won't come to that."

"It might. And if it does, you'd better be ready to make the hard choice."

Amelia emerged from her bedroom with a suitcase and her purse, her laptop bag slung over her shoulder. She'd changed into jeans, boots, and a beaten-up leather jacket. But that wasn't all she'd changed, with there now being a determined set to her jaw that told me she wasn't backing down.

"Ready," she said, her gaze flickering between Chase and me.

"Are you sure about coming with us? I'd rather

drive you back to my place, where you'll be safe. There's still time."

"Mal, someone broke into my home, stole my files, and tried to intimidate me. I want to know who, and I want to know why." She again looked between Chase and me. "And I want to help catch them in the act."

Chase grinned. "Yeah, I like her."

As we loaded her bag into my truck, I caught myself scanning the street, checking shadows for movement. The protective instincts I'd developed over the years of dangerous work now belonged to the woman beside me.

"Before we go any farther," Amelia said as we drove through the quiet streets of Coogan's Break, "I want you to tell me everything. Who you are, what it was you used to do, and why Chase thinks someone might use me to target you."

"Amelia..."

"Everything, Mal. No more half-truths or evasions. I heard what Chase said, and if I'm going to be in danger because of your past, I deserve to know what I'm facing."

She was right, of course. If my old life had caught up with me, if someone was using her to get to me, she had every right to know.

But telling her the truth meant risking everything. It meant admitting things that could send me to prison, or worse. It meant revealing a part of myself that I'd spent three years trying to forget.

"After the surveillance," I said. "Once we're back at my place and I know you're safe. Then I'll tell you everything."

"Promise?"

"I promise."

But as I said the words, I wondered if I was about to destroy the best thing that had ever happened to me. Some truths were too dangerous to share, even with the people you cared for deeply.

Then, as if to back this up, my phone buzzed with a text from a number I hadn't seen in over three years:

> Network compromised. Maintain radio silence. Stay alert.

The timing couldn't be worse. Just when I'd found something worth protecting, my past was stirring to life.

And I realized I felt more for Amelia than any woman to date. Which made what I had to tell her even more terrifying.

EIGHT

AMELIA

The drive to the warehouse felt surreal. Less than two hours ago, I'd been curled up on my couch with a book.

Now I was sitting in Malakai's truck with my suitcase in the back, my cottage a crime scene, and my sense of safety shattered.

"You're sure about this surveillance idea?" I asked Malakai as we turned into the historic district. "I mean, what if they turn up?"

"If they do, it won't be for a while yet," said Malakai with quiet certainty. "They'll be expecting us to call the cops like normal people, leaving them the best part of the night to get organized. We've got time to get everything set up."

Soon enough, we were parking as close as we dared

to the warehouse, with Chase's truck coming to a stop behind us. However, rather than stay put as we were, he jumped out and locked his cab.

I then watched as he leaned over the bed of his truck and retrieved what looked like military-grade equipment bags. The sight should have been reassuring, but instead it drove home how far out of my depth I was.

"This feels like something from a movie," I said.

"Relax, we'll be fine. Most surveillance is boring enough to warrant a GA rating," said Malakai with a snort. "Hours of waiting for nothing to happen."

I studied the warehouse in the moonlight. The building that had represented hope and family legacy now felt ominous, full of shadows and secrets. "I can't believe someone trashed my Airbnb because of this place."

I was still thinking about it when Malakai lowered his window, allowing the cool night air to worm its way inside the cab. When Chase hunkered down next to the truck, the smell of the city was soon replaced by expensive aftershave.

"After that break-in, we need to rethink our approach," said Chase.

His not looking at me when he said this told me he didn't expect me to contribute to any revisions. Which he wasn't wrong about. All I knew was that other than the basic security system I'd invested in, the warehouse was ripe for the picking.

As luck would have it, Malakai was able to go into more detail for the bounty hunter. "Basic off-the-shelf alarm system, and a couple of new keycard locks," he said. "There's also a security camera at the main entrance, but it's ancient and I doubt it's connected." When he glanced in my direction, I shook my head, all while berating myself for my lack of planning.

Chase's expression told me without words what he thought of my current security system, with system perhaps a bit of a stretch. "Amelia, we'll need to set up our own monitoring if that's okay with you? Mal and I can place some wireless cameras with night-vision capability. Nothing permanent, nothing that will damage the building."

"If that's the case," I said, leaning forward in my seat so I could look Chase in the eye, "why do you need my permission?"

"Because it's your building," said Malakai, answering on behalf of the other man. "We're not doing anything without your say-so."

The courtesy felt strange after weeks of people trying to block, buy, or undermine my renovation. "What are you planning?"

Malakai reached down the side of his seat and retrieved a tablet with the floor plan I'd given him earlier, soon up on screen. "Our original plan was to watch the warehouse from across the road, but after tonight, we need a better handle on things than that."

With Chase now leaning in the window, the men took a fresh look at the building, one that would have the warehouse bristling with surveillance equipment.

"I reckon we go with motion-activated cameras here, here, and here," said Mal, pointing to key locations.

"We'll need audio pickup near the main entrances. And remote monitoring from up there," said Chase when Malakai swiped through to the second-floor where I'd established my temporary office.

On seeing Mal was about to carry on, I rested my hand on his arm to stop him. "How long will this take to set up?"

"An hour, maybe two," he said. "We'll need access to power outlets, plus I'll also need to set up a Wi-Fi modem."

I thought about it, with the logical part of my brain saying this was crazy. Why were we playing spy games instead of calling the police? Then it came to me in a flash. The break-in at my cottage had been too clean, too professional. Whoever was behind this had resources and connections.

Just because the holds on my permits had been lifted, that didn't mean there wasn't someone else in local government who, for whatever reason, was out to have me fail. And if that happened, then whoever was out to get me would swoop in and get the warehouse at a knockdown price. "Do it," I said, looking at Mal and Chase in turn. "But I want to know what you're installing and where."

"Fair enough," said Chase. "And after tonight, if we don't catch anyone, you'll still need to make yourself scarce until further notice."

"Meaning?" I said, my gut already telling me what he was hinting at.

"Meaning you stay with Mal until this is resolved," said Chase, his tone brooking no argument. "Your cottage isn't secure enough, and a hotel could be worse."

I looked at Malakai, glad the cab of the truck was dark enough to hide my blush. "Are you okay with that?" I wasn't comfortable having myself foisted on him like this. It was one thing to stay overnight, but who knew how long it might take to catch those behind the break-in.

Sure, Mal and I had connected on a physical level, but other than that, we were strangers. What if I took up too much space for him? What if he proved himself a slob? There was no quicker way to take the shine off a fledgling romance than to be in close quarters with someone.

"Lia, I want you safe, no matter how long it takes. We can figure out everything else as we go."

The certainty in his voice made something warm unfurl in my chest, even as my practical side rebelled against being driven from my own space.

"We'll see how tonight goes," I said.

Chase grinned. "She's stubborn."

"Yeah," said Malakai, but there was affection in his voice. "I noticed."

Inside the warehouse, I watched Chase and Malakai work with professional efficiency. The cameras and motion sensors were small, only just visible once positioned, with the whole setup more sophisticated than anything I'd expected.

"Military surplus?" I asked, looking at the camo bag of equipment Malakai had retrieved from the back of his own truck.

"Something like that," said Chase with a chuckle. "The important thing is that it's better than what you had, and even better is that they won't be expecting it."

I was about to ask if it was legal, then decided that I didn't give a damn if it was. Not after how scared I'd been thanks to that intruder.

"It's your building, and you're not recording anyone without their knowledge in a public space," said Malakai. "Plus, we're investigating crimes that have already been committed against you, so we're all good."

"You sound like you've done this before," I said, looking at him in a new light. In this case, it was the narrow beam of a flashlight.

But before he could answer, his phone vibrated. His jaw tightened almost imperceptibly after he'd checked it, with me straightening in response.

"Mal?"

"It's nothing," he said, but his voice had an edge I hadn't heard before. "Just an old contact checking in." He pocketed the phone quickly. "Sometimes it takes a while for the dust to settle."

His answer felt vague, but I didn't push. Everyone had a past, although I suspected his was more colorful than most.

Even so, I filed this latest avoidance away with all his others. He'd promised to tell me everything once we were back at his place, and I intended to hold him to it.

As he and Chase worked together setting up the surveillance equipment, I watched the way Malakai's hands moved. Confident, precise, and gentle with the delicate electronics, just as he was with me.

There was something mesmerizing about his competence, but more than that, I liked how he explained what he was doing, making sure I understood rather than leaving me in the dark.

"You're good at this," I said as he adjusted a camera angle.

"Practice," he replied, glancing at me, something soft in his expression. "Most people don't want to understand. They just want the problem solved."

"I'm not most people."

"No," he said, his voice quiet. "You're not."

There was something in that moment. Not just attraction or adrenaline, but recognition. Like we fit together in ways that had nothing to do with circumstance and everything to do with who we were when we weren't trying to impress each other.

It made me think this could work. Really work.

Because of this, my heart had been in my mouth when he leaned out of the top-floor windows so he could install cameras outside. Even though I knew my hanging onto his legs wouldn't stop him from falling if he slipped, I felt better doing so.

It was just under two hours when Malakai and Chase declared they were ready to leave, which rather took me by surprise. I'd expected us to hide out on the top floor, but the men had other ideas.

"There's not a snowball's chance in hell we want to risk being trapped up there," said Chase. "Just because there was only one guy at your place, chances are he won't want to tackle a building this big on his own."

Mal then added his two cents worth. "Also, we don't know how long it'll take them to go through the thumb drives they stole from you. We may as well be comfortable while we wait."

Why did I keep forgetting that part of the proceedings? That's right, because I was an architect, not whatever these two were. "So how will we know if they break in?"

A moment later, Malakai held his tablet aloft, the screen now split into a series of small boxes, with each representing a camera. Then Chase held up his own tablet with floor plans of the building showing a series of green flashing lights.

Presumably, if the motion sensors were tripped, the green would soon change to red. At least, that made the most sense to me. But what did I know?

With the surveillance equipment installed, we jumped back in Malakai's truck, but rather than stay put, we reversed out of the alleyway. "If they see us parked back here, they won't take the bait," he said, turning the truck around and driving a distance down the street.

Likewise, Chase had done the same, only in the other direction. It was now time for us to hunker down and wait, even if relaxation wasn't possible. The atmosphere felt different. More professional, more tense.

. . .

Tucked up against Mal's side with his arm wrapped around me, I was close to falling asleep when I felt him tense. That we had company was soon backed up by Chase.

"We've got company," he said, his voice crackling through the radio he'd given Malakai. "Two vehicles approaching from the north."

My pulse jumped. "Are we sure they're coming here?"

"They're moving without lights," said Mal, his eyes now glued to his tablet. "And they're the first vehicles we've seen all night."

On the screen, I watched two dark SUVs turn into the alleyway that ran around the back of the building. While they were now hidden from the street, the cameras Mal had installed earlier meant we could still see what they were up to.

"No hesitation," he observed. "They've done reconnaissance."

"How many people?" I asked, my fingers crossed that there was only one per vehicle.

"Hard to tell with the tinted windows," said Mal, holding the tablet between us so I could more easily see what was going on. "But based on how the vehicles are sitting... at least four, maybe six in each truck."

My mouth went dry. "That's more people than you'd need for a simple break-in." It didn't take me long to realize that it was also a lot more than Chase and Mal could handle on their own.

"There's nothing simple about this," said Malakai. "For there to be this many guys on hand, they had to have been planning it from before they broke into your place."

While one SUV stopped near the side entrance, the other continued around to the loading dock, with the coordination both obvious and unsettling.

"They know the layout," Chase's voice came through the radio. "No hesitation. They've either been here before, or they have inside information."

"Inside information from where?" I said, genuinely confused.

"I doubt they've had time to go through all those thumb drives," said Mal, "which tells me it's courtesy of the planning department. They'd have copies of all your building documentation, including original blueprints."

On screen, figures emerged from the vehicles. Even in the grainy night vision, their movements showed them to be part of a tight-knit team.

"Six people confirmed, both vehicles," reported Chase. "And they're carrying equipment cases. Heavy-duty crap, by the look of things."

I watched in horror as strangers approached the warehouse with unknown intentions, anger burning through my fear. "I want to know who the hell they are."

"You will," said Malakai, "but in the meantime, we stay safe and we stay smart. Document everything and get evidence. Only then can we figure out our next step."

"Our next step should be calling the police."

"With what evidence? They haven't broken in yet, and between Chase and me, we're better placed to move if we don't have to worry about red tape."

He was right, and I hated it. I watched six of the intruders approach the side entrance, but instead of picking the lock, the lead figure used a key card. A moment later and the six crowding around the loading dock entered using the same method.

"They have authorized access," I whispered, unable to believe what I was seeing. "That's impossible. I'm the only one with ..." I stopped, remembering the planning department weasel who'd tried to discourage me from the renovation. "Unless someone copied my access codes when they had my documentation."

"Your friend from the planning department?"

"He's not my friend. And if he's involved in this, I'm going to make sure he regrets it."

The intruders moved through the warehouse with confidence, their powerful LED lights cutting through the darkness. They headed straight to my office on the top floor and the old-fashioned plan drawers where I kept my architectural plans and research materials.

"They know what they're looking for," I said, watching them comb through every drawer in the antique unit.

"And where to find it," added Malakai. "It looks like someone's been feeding them detailed information."

I watched as the intruders photographed my plans, my research, my family's history, with the violation feeling personal in a way the cottage break-in hadn't. The only difference here was that they didn't scatter all my papers around as they had at the Airbnb.

"So, what's the plan?" I asked. "We can't just sit here and watch them steal whatever they're after."

"Like I said, we document everything," said Mal. "Get evidence of who they are and what they're doing. Then we figure out how to stop them."

"And if they find whatever they're looking for?"

"Then we'll deal with that, too," he said. "But right now, our priority is keeping you safe and gathering intelligence."

On the monitors, the search team had moved through the main floor and was now heading to the basement level. They were using some kind of scanning equipment, working through the foundation structure.

"Metal detectors?" I asked.

"More sophisticated than that," piped up Chase. "Looks like ground-penetrating radar. If there's anything hidden in the walls or foundation, that equipment should find it."

All of a sudden, those family stories didn't seem like folklore anymore. "You think there's gold hidden in the building?"

"I think someone believes there is," said Mal. "And they're willing to go to considerable trouble to find it."

"Mal," Chase's voice crackled through the radio. "They just found something. Basement, north wall. Both teams are converging."

On screen, I could see the excitement in their body language as they gathered around their scanning equipment. Whatever they'd found had them animated, pointing and gesturing.

"I want to know what they've discovered," I said.

"So do I," replied Malakai. "But we'd be stupid to take on twelve guys on our own."

I absorbed this, watching strangers make themselves at home in the building my family had owned for over a century. The weight of generations of secrets and betrayals pressed down on me.

A soft alarm chimed from the tablet, and Chase's voice came through the radio. "They're wrapping up. Whatever they were hunting for, it looks like they got it."

On screen, the team was packing up their equipment, moving with the same efficiency they'd shown during the search.

"What do we do now?" I asked.

"Now we follow them," said Mal, starting the truck's engine. "Find out where they're based, who they're working for."

"Is that safe?"

"Safer than letting them disappear with whatever they've discovered," he said. "We stay back, we stay alert, and we find out who's behind this." He then used the radio to communicate with Chase.

"Chase, can you stay on watch while we follow?"

"Negative. We need two for the tail. But we've got motion alerts on our phones. If anyone else turns up, we can give Daemon and the others a call."

"All right," I said, doing up my seatbelt and settling back in my seat. "Let's see where this leads."

NINE

MALAKAI

Following two SUVs through the back streets of Coogan's Break at midnight was nothing like the spy thriller Amelia seemed to think it was. Instead, it was a dangerous game of cat and mouse where I wasn't sure which roles we were playing.

"They're splitting up," I said, watching the lead vehicle take a right turn while the second continued straight. "Chase, you take the one going north. We'll follow the other."

"Copy that," Chase's voice crackled through the radio. "Stay back, don't get made."

Easier said than done. The SUV we were tailing seemed to know where it was going, taking turns with confidence through residential neighborhoods I wasn't familiar with. Beside me, Amelia gripped the door handle as I navigated the winding streets, trying to maintain visual contact without getting close enough to be spotted.

"They're heading toward the industrial district," observed Amelia, studying the route on my tablet's GPS. "It doesn't appear there's much out that way except warehouses. It says here, an abandoned mining operation."

"That makes sense. Somewhere they can get up to no good without neighbors asking questions."

We followed for another ten minutes, during which time the SUV maintained a steady pace, suggesting they weren't in any hurry. Which made it all the more jarring when the pavement ended, the dirt began, and the vehicle took off. This left us choking in a cloud of dust, with no option but to slow to a crawl.

"Fuck," I muttered, waiting for the dust to dissipate so I could follow without risking going off the road.

And if that wasn't bad enough, when we hit a crossroads, the amount of dust still hanging in the air made it impossible to know which way they'd gone. The cloud was also dense enough that they must have spun their wheels, telling me they knew they were being followed. Or they were speeding for the sheer hell of it.

"We lost them." said Amelia, her gaze also locked on the temporary dust storm.

"Yeah, damn it," I said, easing in next to a derelict shack and killing the headlights. "And there's no way we're going in blind. Not if there's a chance they know we're on to them." I'd learned my lesson on that in the past and wasn't about to repeat it, especially not with Amelia beside me.

She slumped back in her seat, as frustrated as I was. "So much for gathering intelligence."

"Hey, we got more than we expected. We know they're organized, well-equipped, and they found something at the warehouse. We just need to work out what." I picked up the radio. "Chase, come in. What's your status?"

Static answered me.

"Chase, do you copy?"

More static followed before his voice came through, loud and clear. "Yeah, I'm here. Still got eyes on my target. They pulled into a compound about three miles north of downtown. Looks like a legitimate business front."

After taking in our surroundings, I gave him an update on our situation. "We're out in the boonies, complete with dirt roads and rotting buildings. Even if we knew which way they went, there's not a chance I want to keep tailing them."

Following more crackling, Chase responded. "You're all good, mate."

"Any chance of getting an address so we can join you?" I asked him.

While Chase didn't respond in words, a minute later my phone buzzed with an incoming message. Chase had sent a link to a location pin on a mapping app, along with coordinates, a street address, and even a link to a website.

"Bingo," I said, showing Amelia the screen. "Looks like a freight forwarding company. Perfect cover when you don't want to attract attention."

"So now what?" She asked, looking at me with wide eyes. "Do we call the police?"

Before I could answer, the radio crackled to life. "Mal, whatever you do, don't head this way. I've got a visual on at least eight guys plus the six that were in the SUV. And I've seen more firepower than I'm comfortable with. I'm getting out of here."

"Copy that. We're heading back to my place. Speak to you in the morning."

With this in mind, I tossed my phone into Amelia's lap and took off. We were back on the outskirts of town when I heard her gasp, with this enough to have me pulling over to see what was wrong.

However, rather than looking upset, she held my phone up, with it taking me a second to comprehend the map wasn't showing Chase's location. "How in the hell did he manage..."

I didn't even have time to finish my thought or get Chase on the radio when he beat me to it.

"I may have slapped tracking devices on both vehicles while the teams were in the basement at the warehouse." There was no missing the note of satisfaction in Chase's voice, and I suspected there was a broad grin that went along with it.

Even so, I stared at the radio for a moment. How had I missed his doing that? I was out of practice, that was for sure, and that worried me. A lot. At least enough to have me second-guessing myself.

"I figured an insurance policy wouldn't go amiss," said Chase, interrupting my self-reflection. "My little beauties will tell us where those trucks go for the next week, assuming nobody finds the gizmos. They're pretty freaking small."

What wasn't small was the way Amelia was looking at me, with her expression wavering between admiration and disbelief. "Is that even legal?"

"Maybe not," I said. "But neither is breaking into the warehouse with professional equipment."

"Damn right," Chase's voice came through. "These assholes want to play hardball, we'll play hardball. But not tonight. Too many of them, too well armed. We regroup and plan our next move."

"Agreed," I said. "We'll meet you back at the warehouse in the morning."

"Make it in the afternoon. I want to get some sleep before we figure out what in the hell those people found tonight."

I fired up the truck again and started back toward my place, aware of Amelia studying me in the dim light from the dashboard.

"You're nervous," she said.

"About what?"

"Taking me to your place. You keep checking the mirrors, adjusting your grip on the steering wheel. Either you think we're still being followed, or you're worried about something else."

She was observant. Too observant. "It's not what you'd call homey."

"I'm not looking for homey, Mal. I'm looking for safety. And answers."

The answers. Right. I'd promised to tell her everything once we got back to my place, and the time for evasions was over. The woman had watched a gang of low-life scum ransack her family's building. She deserved to know what kind of man she was trusting with her safety.

. . .

My house was nondescript, double-story with a walk-in basement, neutral siding, nothing flashy. It was also on the wrong side of town, chosen because it was the sort of place most folks avoided. It was also the sort of neighborhood where anyone official stood out like a sore thumb.

But the landscaping told a different story if you knew what to look for. Hardscrabble instead of grass, motion-activated security lights positioned at strategic intervals, and clear sight lines in every direction.

"This is it," I said, pulling into the driveway and hitting the remote for the garage door.

Only after I'd pulled into the garage and shut the door behind us did Amelia climb out of the truck. She looked around the space, taking in the workbenches that lined the walls, and the tool cabinets that stood at precise intervals. As with everything in my life, it was organized with military precision.

"It's very... neat," she said with care.

"Wait until you see upstairs."

The living space occupied the second floor, accessible by a steel staircase that echoed under our feet. It had been designed for function over form with the added advantage that it was fireproof.

There was nothing home and garden about the living area with its open floor plan, minimal furniture, and clear sight lines to all entrances. Meanwhile, the windows were bulletproof, and the doors were reinforced steel.

"Wow," said Amelia, taking in the spartan environment and the discrete cameras that looked down from every corner of the room. "You weren't kidding about the security."

"Motion sensors, reinforced everything, communications equipment that would make some government departments jealous." As if to back this up, I gestured toward a bank of monitors that sat alongside the small but functional kitchenette. "Like I said, not homey."

She walked to the center of the room, turning to take it all in. "It's the home of someone who's been running for a long time."

"Three years, two months, and sixteen days," I said. "Not that I'm counting."

"And now?"

"Now I need to tell you why I've been running, and then it's up to you to decide whether you still want my help." I moved to the kitchen and pulled out a bottle of whiskey. "You need a drink for this?"

"I want the truth."

Fair enough. I poured myself two fingers of bourbon and took a sip, buying time to figure out where to start.

"My real name is Malcolm Tremaine." The words

felt foreign to me. I hadn't spoken that name aloud in three years, two months, and sixteen days.

My hands shook, so I gripped the bourbon glass tighter. "Three years ago, I was working on a mission that went pear-shaped."

I had to stop, close my eyes, force myself to breathe. The smell of burning diesel and cordite filled my nostrils as if I were back there. "The target was supposed to be a terrorist cell. That's what they told us. What they told me."

"Mal?" Amelia's voice seemed to come from far away. I opened my eyes, focusing on her face to anchor myself in the present.

"Sorry. Sometimes it feels like yesterday. The whistleblower was a pediatrician turned government translator. He'd discovered contracts were being funneled to companies that didn't exist, millions disappearing while soldiers went without proper equipment."

My voice cracked. "He had a daughter. Eight years old. She was... she was in the car when... I submitted a report detailing what had happened, thinking my superiors would want to know. Instead, they tried pinning the deaths on me."

"And your superiors, did they have the right of it?" asked Amelia, her face ashen.

"Hell no! I avoided that, thank God. Not that it

counted for much when my bosses made up their minds to blame the fuck-up on me. So, I faked my death, erased my identity, and disappeared." I set down the glass and looked at her. "I've been hiding ever since, using forged documents, staying off the grid, working jobs that don't require background checks."

"Like Lucky Break Construction?"

"Ethan took a chance on me when nobody else would. He needed someone with security experience, and I needed work that would keep me invisible."

"Invisible?" she said while twirling a make-believe mustache. "You're hardly flying under the radar with that thing."

"Hah, you'd be surprised. Hiding in plain sight can be incredibly effective. People who are doing their best to blend into the background often make themselves more obvious because of it."

I followed this up by doing some twirling of my own and was relieved to see laughter sparkling in Amelia's eyes. "The job at Lucky Break was only supposed to be a temporary gig."

"But it didn't end up that way, did it?"

"No. Turns out I enjoy building things more than I ever enjoyed tearing them down." I moved to the window, checking the street out of habit. "But that's my life, Amelia. I can't get a legitimate contractor's license, can't establish credit, can't even see a doctor without using fake ID. For all intents and purposes, I'm dead, disconnected, don't exist."

"And what about relationships?"

Her question caught me off guard. "What?"

"Relationships. What's your situation with those?"

I turned to look at her, trying to read her expression. "It's never come up before?"

"And yet here we are."

"Yeah, here we are," I agreed. "Which is why I should walk away. The last thing you need is to be around if my past catches up with me."

She stood up, crossed the room, and stopped right in front of me. "But you won't leave, will you?"

"No. I won't."

"Why?"

Again, I was thrown. Why was I sticking around? Perhaps because she was the first person in three years who'd made me feel like I might have a future. Or because when I was with her, I forgot about being dead and remembered what it felt like to be alive. As it was, the thought of someone hurting her had me wanting to tear the world apart with my bare hands.

Of course, I said none of that. Rather, I chickened out and said, "I'm staying, because I gave you my word."

She studied my face for a long moment, then reached up and stroked the side of my face. "That's not the only reason."

"No," I admitted. "It's not."

"Good," she said, and kissed me.

What happened next confirmed every fear I'd had about getting involved with someone while living under a false identity. Because making love to Amelia Donovan wasn't just physical. It was a claiming, a surrender, a promise I had no right to make but couldn't stop myself from giving.

She stripped away more than just my clothes. She stripped away the careful emotional distance I'd maintained for three years, the professional detachment that had kept me sane, the barriers I'd built to protect others.

And when she fell asleep in my arms afterward, her head on my chest and her breathing soft and even, I lay awake staring at the ceiling and wondering if I'd just made the biggest mistake of my life. Or the best decision.

The next morning dawned gray and cold, with Amelia making coffee in my utilitarian kitchen while I checked the overnight surveillance feeds from the warehouse. Nothing had happened. There'd been no return visits, no additional searches, no signs that our midnight adventure had been detected.

"Any word from Chase?" she asked, handing me a mug.

"He texted an hour ago. Everything's quiet at the compound. The tracking devices are still active, so we'll know if those vehicles move."

"And our next step?"

"We meet the team at the warehouse, see if we can figure out what those people found in your basement." I pulled her close, and buried my nose in her hair, the delicate scent arousing me as always. "Only then can we decide how to proceed."

She looked up at me with those dark eyes that had been haunting my dreams. "Any regrets about last night?"

"About the surveillance? No. About bringing you into this mess? Yes." I kissed her forehead. "About what happened between us? Never."

"Good answer," she said before taking a sip of her coffee.

We arrived at the warehouse to find Ethan's truck already parked outside, along with vehicles belonging to Tyler and Daemon. The team was gathered in the basement, studying the north wall with the intensity of archaeologists examining an ancient artifact.

"Find anything interesting?" I called out as we descended the stairs.

"That's what we're trying to figure out," said Ethan. "Whatever those people were looking for, I think they came close to finding it. Look at this."

He pointed to a section of wall where the mortar between the stones had recently been disturbed. "Apart from some surface work, they marked the stone with chalk? That tells me they knew where to focus the equipment Chase told me about."

Tyler looked up from where he was examining the stonework. "Question is, what were they looking for? And did they find it?"

"Or did they strike out altogether and we're looking at a repeat performance?" added Daemon. "Because if I'm being honest, my Saturday mornings are often more predictable than this."

Before anyone could answer, we heard footsteps on the stairs. A moment later, Cole Stillman appeared. As well as being uncle to Zac Thomas, he was another Lucky Break team member, although I'd yet to find out what his role was.

When I'd first started with Lucky Break, I'd had a dig around, but it was like trying to pin down smoke. Then Zac and Ethan told me to leave it be, that the guy could be trusted, and I should give it a rest.

Cole had also been around long enough to have opinions about everything.

While I took the time to introduce him to Amelia, I gave thought to the guy's sudden appearance. With Zac working on another project, I was surprised to see him there. It was more usual for him to turn up only when his nephew was around.

And then I had a reality check. How often in the past had he turned up when things were getting interesting? Too often to be deemed a coincidence, that was for damned sure.

"Zac told me you folks had some excitement last night," he said, looking around the group and confirming my suspicions. "Figured I'd come look at whatever's got everyone stirred up."

Supposedly, Cole was able to read situations the way other people read books. He was also known for being downright scary when the situation called for it, with the type of street smarts that suggested a colorful past. If anyone could figure out what the intruders were after or had discovered, it would be him.

"What's your take on it?" said Ethan, gesturing toward the marked section of wall.

Cole pulled out a pair of reading glasses, which somewhat ruined his street cred, before proceeding to examine the stonework.

"Interesting. This part of the wall looks to have been completed later. The stone isn't quite the same, and the mortar's different, too."

"Meaning?" said Amelia, peering at the spot Cole was pointing to.

"Meaning it was added later," he said to her. "And whoever built it wanted it to blend in."

"So, what's behind the wall?" asked Tyler.

"There's only one way to find out," said Cole. "but I'd recommend doing it with care. If you swing sledgehammers at a century-old stonework, you might bring down more than you bargained for."

Amelia and I exchanged glances. "We'll let you guys handle the archaeological investigation," I said, looking around the rest of the team. "We need to check Amelia's office, make sure nothing was disturbed up there."

Although that wasn't all I wanted. I also wanted a few minutes alone with her to discuss what we'd learned and plan our next move. The basement was getting crowded, and I thought better when I wasn't surrounded by those offering helpful opinions.

Upstairs, Amelia's office looked as we'd left it the night before. The intruders had photographed everything but had taken nothing physical. She moved to the window that offered a view of the historic district, the morning light highlighting the determined set of her jaw.

"They're going to find something down there, aren't they?" she said.

"I reckon they will. The bottom line is whether it's what those people were looking for, or just the tip of the iceberg."

She looked at me over her shoulder. "And when we find whatever it is?"

"Then we'll know why someone would mount a professional operation to search your building." I moved behind her, wrapping my arms around her waist and resting my chin atop her head. "And we'll figure out how to protect both you and whatever your ancestors left behind."

She leaned back against me, and I could feel some of the tension leave her body. "I keep thinking about last night. Not just what we learned, but..." She trailed off.

"What happened between us?"

"Yeah. It changes things, doesn't it?"

"Everything," I agreed. "For better or worse."

She turned in my arms, snuggling against my chest. "For better. Doubtless for better."

I was about to kiss her when the building shook.

Not the gentle settling of old stone and timber, but

a sharp, violent jerk that rattled the windows and sent dust cascading from the ceiling beams.

"Earthquake?" said Amelia, holding onto me as if preparing for an aftershock.

I thought back to the quality of the sound, and the way it had echoed through the building's structure. "No. That came from the basement."

We looked at each other for one frozen moment, then raced for the stairs.

We were met with chaos. Dust filled the air, making it hard to see, with the sound of falling blocks still echoing through the space. When the haze cleared somewhat, I could make out figures moving near the north wall.

"Ethan!" I called out. "Is everyone okay?"

"Over here!" yelled Tyler. "Ethan's down!"

We reached the north wall to find Ethan lying motionless on the ground, covered in broken stone and dust. Cole, Daemon, and Tyler were already kneeling beside him, easing debris to the side and checking for injuries.

"Don't move him," Cole instructed as Daemon helped Ethan sit up. "Could be internal injuries."

"I'm fine," said Ethan, his breathing strained. "Just got the wind knocked out of me when the wall came down."

"The wall came down?" said Amelia, shocked.

"Yeah," said Tyler, getting to his knees to examine the damaged stonework. "We hardly touched it. But I guess whoever built it was in a hurry to cover what they were up to. More concerned about getting the job done than structural integrity."

Through the settling dust, I could see that a section of the north wall had indeed collapsed, revealing a dark cavity.

"Fuck me," said Daemon, forgetting both Ethan and his manners in his excitement. "There has to be something back there."

Not willing to miss out on any excitement, Cole already had one foot through the breach, ignoring warnings from the others about structural instability. "Hand me that flashlight," he called back to Daemon.

"Cole, if that wall's compromised—" protested Ethan, still struggling to breathe.

"I'll be fine," said the older man, shining the light into the gloom. "Any dodgy stonework is history. And the rest is as solid as the day it was built."

He then disappeared into the opening, although we could hear him moving around. A moment later, his voice came back to us, thick with excitement.

"Well, I'll be damned."

"What is it?" called out Amelia.

Cole reappeared, dust-covered and grinning like a man who'd just struck gold, which I suspected wasn't too far from the truth. In his hands was a canvas bag, old and stained but intact.

"Looks like those family tales Zac told me about weren't folklore after all, Miss Amelia," said Cole, hefting the bag and leaving me wondering how he'd heard the stories.

He then loosened the drawstring and tilted the bag so we could all see inside. Even in the dim basement light, there was no mistaking the bright gleam of gold.

"How much?" asked Amelia, her voice not much above a whisper.

"Hard to say without weighing it, but I'd guess a half-a-pound, maybe even more." Cole retied the bag and handed it to her. "Congratulations, Miss Amelia. At the current rate, that's got to be around thirty or forty grand."

I watched Amelia hold the bag, seeing a mix of emotions cross her face. Excitement, disbelief, and something that looked like fear. It was the last that damned near brought me to my knees.

"This is what they were after," she said. "This is why they broke into my cottage, why they searched the warehouse."

"Could be," I said, studying the collapsed wall, and the hidden space beyond. "But is this all of it, or is there more?"

Because if there was one cache of gold hidden in

the warehouse walls, there might be more. And if those people knew about it, they'd be back.

Even putting the building's structural integrity to one side, the game had just gotten a lot more dangerous.

TEN

AMELIA

The weight of the gold in my hands felt heavier than Cole's estimate suggested. Not because of the metal itself, but because of what it represented. It was confirmation that everything I'd dismissed as family folklore was true. And if the stories about hidden gold were real, then the stories about betrayal and murder doubtless were too.

"We need to get this somewhere safe," said Malakai, taking the canvas bag from me and hefting it as if to check the weight for himself. "And then we need to figure out who we're dealing with."

"I don't have a safe deposit box," I said. "I've never needed one before."

"My place has a gun safe. Military grade, fireproof,

the works." He studied my face in the dusty basement light. "Unless you'd rather take it to a bank?"

I thought about walking into Coogan's Break First National with a bag of century-old gold, trying to explain where it came from and why I needed to store it. "Your safe sounds perfect."

The drive back to Malakai's house felt different from the night before. Then I'd been a wreck thanks to the break-in at my cottage and anxious over what I was to hear about his past.

Now, I was grappling with the reality that my family's building contained hidden treasure in volumes such that professional criminals would kill for it.

"You're quiet," observed Malakai as we pulled into his garage.

"I'm trying to wrap my head around all of this. Yesterday, the biggest decision I had to make was whether to use subway tile or natural stone in the renovated bathrooms. Today, I'm hiding gold and dodging armed treasure hunters."

"Welcome to my old world," he said with a grim smile. "Though it was rare for the people shooting at me to be after gold."

Inside his fortress-like house, I watched him open a safe that looked like it could survive a nuclear blast. The gold disappeared inside, along with what looked like several weapons, cash, and documents I didn't recognize.

"There," he said, spinning the dial. "Safe as it gets."

"Now what?"

"Now we figure out who's behind this." He moved to his bank of monitors and computers. "Starting with that freight forwarding company Chase found."

I settled beside him as he pulled up multiple screens, his fingers flying over the keyboard with the efficiency of someone who'd done this many times. Within minutes, he had corporate records, property listings, and what looked like financial reports spread across three monitors.

"Interesting," he said, pointing to the business registration. "Company was founded eighteen months ago. Minimal staff, and their client list is... sparse."

"A front?"

"Has to be. Look at this," he said, pointing to the left-hand screen. "They're paying rent on a facility that could handle major shipping operations, but their declared revenue wouldn't cover utilities." He switched to another screen. "Owner is listed as MC Enterprises. Let me dig deeper."

I watched him work, making notes on a legal pad. There was something mesmerizing about his focus, the way he could sift through layers of information and spot the patterns that mattered.

His concentration was broken only when his phone rang, the ringtone not one I recognized, although he did, with him hesitating rather than answering it straight off as he always would. It was only when he had the phone up to his ear that I realized it wasn't his usual one.

"Torres." A pause. "When?... How deep?... Understood."

He hung up, his expression grim.

"What was that about?" I asked.

"Someone's been asking questions about me. The kind that attracts attention from people I'd rather leave sleeping." He met my eyes. "I've been digging around, following money trails, tracing shell companies, crap like that. But the tools I used aren't civilian-grade."

"Meaning?"

"Meaning, when you access certain databases without proper authorization, it can send up flags. And they can alert those who might recognize my digital signature."

As if this didn't raise more questions than it answered, he then got back to searching for anything that would point us in the right direction.

"Got something," he said twenty minutes later. "MC Enterprises is owned by James Holdings, which is owned by..." He paused, highlighting a name on the screen. "Margaret Quinn."

"Damn it! I'd never even heard of the blasted woman until last week. And now every time I turn around, she's there. There has to be some connection to my family or the warehouse. Otherwise, why would she target me?"

While Mal continued looking for online clues, I tried to remember the tales my grandfather had told me when I was a little kid. "Jeremiah Donovan and James Campbell owned the Lucky Strike mine together. Anyway, they found gold, lots of it by all accounts, but then James died without warning. The story goes he was trying to cheat Jeremiah out of his share, and he found out about it."

Mal glanced at me before once again concentrating on the screen. "Then who's Margaret Quinn in all of this..."

"Maybe a descendant." I said without conviction.

"Let's find out." Malakai pulled up another screen and typed into the search engine, with a screed of information showing up a second later. "Margaret Quinn, age seventy-three, longtime Coogan's Break resident. Owns property throughout the area, including..." He whistled low. "The Lucky Strike mine."

While scrolling down the page looking for anything else of note, he added, "That's the second address Chase sent through last night. It'd be the perfect place to plan operations without neighbors asking questions." With his eyes still locked on the screen, he switched to a local newspaper website. "Let me check the archives, see what kind of community involvement she has."

The Coogan's Break Gazette had been digitizing its old issues, but many of the older articles were still only available on microfiche. Malakai printed out a list of references to Margaret Quinn, and we spent the next hour poring over articles dating back forty years.

"Look at this pattern," I said, spreading printouts across his coffee table. "She buys historic properties, applies for renovation permits, and then tears them down and builds modern developments."

"And gets approval every time," noted Malakai. "That involves influence. Could even be that someone in the mayor's office is helping her."

I was studying a photograph from a society page article about a historic preservation fundraiser when two things had my blood running cold. First, Margaret was standing next to the mayor, and looking very chummy at that. Second, hanging on the wall of what appeared to be an elegant dining room, was a painting I recognized.

"Oh my God," I whispered, my hands shaking.

"What is it?"

"That painting." I pointed to the background in the

photo. "I have the original hanging in my condo back in Redding. It's been in my family for generations. It's a portrait of James and Jeremiah's wives, painted around 1860." I studied Margaret's face in the photograph more closely. "And now I know why she seemed familiar when we ran into her at the planning department. Look at her bone structure, the way she holds herself. She looks just like Sarah Campbell - James's wife in that painting."

Malakai leaned closer to examine the image. "You're sure it's the same painting?"

"Positive. Look at Felicity Donovan's dress, the way she's holding that locket. My grandmother told me stories about that portrait, how it was one of the few things, apart from the warehouse, that the family kept when they lost pretty much everything." My voice dropped to a whisper. "But how does Margaret Quinn have what looks like the same painting?"

"What if it's not the same?" said Malakai, his voice grim. "What if it's a copy? Either way, we need to know where that photograph was taken."

This saw him pulling up more detailed background searches of Margaret Quinn, including a magazine article that featured local historic homes. Within minutes, he'd uncovered birth records, marriage certificates, and Margaret's current address.

"Here we go," he said, highlighting a marriage

certificate. "Margaret Campbell married Robert Quinn in 1985. Campbell was her maiden name."

The pieces clicked into place with sickening clarity. "Campbell," I whispered, having trouble comprehending that the boogeyman of family lore was now knocking on my door.

I'd always assumed the Campbell family line had died out decades ago. With all the marriages and name changes over the generations, and the way both families had scattered after the mining bust, I never imagined there could be any direct descendants left. How wrong I'd been.

"So, Margaret Quinn née Campbell is a relative of James Campbell, your forebear's business partner," said Malakai in summary. "Huh, I guess that explains the James Holdings company name."

I studied the newspaper photo again, noting how Margaret's smile didn't reach her eyes, how she stood with the mayor and city council members like she owned them. "She's not just some random treasure hunter. This is personal."

"I'd say very personal. I also reckon she's been planning this for a long time."

When I gathered up the printouts of the properties that she'd developed and took the time to study them, a cold realization crept over me.

"Mal, look at these properties. The old boarding

house on Elm Street was demolished in 2018. The mercantile building downtown was demolished in 2019. Even the house where my great-grandfather lived was torn down in 2020."

Malakai leaned over my shoulder, studying the list. "To all intents and purposes, she's been destroying your family's legacy."

"Everything but the warehouse. And that's only because the family refused to sell. First my dad, and now me." My hands shook as I held the printouts of the newspaper clippings. "She's been wiping my family off the face of the earth piece by piece."

"Which explains why she's so desperate to get a hold of the warehouse," said Mal, before falling quiet, although not for long. "Aww, geez. Why the hell didn't I see that before? What if, rather than wanting to remove any reference to your family by destroying the buildings, she was more interested in what was under them?"

His comment not only made sense; it had me thinking about my grandfather's stories. About how the family had once owned significant property in Coogan's Break before losing most of it in the economic downturns of the early 1900s.

The warehouse had been all that remained, passed down through generations who couldn't afford to renovate it but couldn't bear to sell it. Toward the end of his days, my grandfather was away with the fairies, with a common refrain being, "They'll keep coming. Keep digging. It's in their blood now." As a child, I'd dismissed it as the ramblings of an old man, but now his words sent a chill down my spine.

"She's not just out to wipe our name from the history books," I said, the full scope of Margaret Quinn's obsession becoming clear. "She's after gold she thinks is hers by right."

It was a thought that had me looking toward Mal's gun locker. There wasn't a chance she could get her greedy paws on it there.

"That must be it. I mean, look at the timeline," said Malakai. "She's been buying up and destroying historic buildings for two decades. But nothing in the last three years."

"Since you came to town?" I said, my mind reeling over how our pasts could have collided thanks to one old lady.

"No, sweet thing, since she started trying to buy your warehouse," he corrected. "Think about all the anonymous offers to purchase it. All turned down by your dad and then you."

I studied yet another photograph from a society page article, with this one about a historic preservation fundraiser. Margaret Quinn stood with the mayor, her smile serene, her silver hair immaculate.

"She looks like someone's sweet grandmother," I said.

"Nah, she looks like someone who'd smile after poisoning your tea," said Malakai, his tone anything but teasing. "I've seen that expression before. More often on people who were very good at getting what they wanted."

"By any means necessary?"

"Yep. No matter how low they had to go," he replied with a definitive nod.

I kept reading, finding more references to Margaret's civic involvement, her donations to local causes, her reputation as a pillar of the community. But between the lines, a different picture emerged. Every property she'd "renovated" had been demolished despite promises to preserve historic features. Every development she'd built had faced minimal opposition from preservation groups.

"She's been playing a long game," I said, glancing at Mal. "Building influence, making connections, positioning herself to get whatever permits she needs."

And I knew I was right about this. Hadn't I had clients do the same thing when they were facing issues with getting planning permission? There was nothing like a few well-placed bribes to oil the wheels of bureaucracy.

"And when she couldn't buy your warehouse, she

tried taking what she wanted by force." Malakai leaned back in his chair. "What worries me more is how much she knows about what else might hide under the warehouse?"

"Enough that they knew where to look last night," I replied, surprised at how angry this thought made me.

I'd only just calmed down and was back looking for more clues among the newspaper articles when my phone buzzed with a text from Chase.

> Still monitoring. Both vehicles now at the compound. No movement since 0600.

"At least we know where they are," I said, showing Malakai the message.

"For now. But they won't stay put forever. Margaret Quinn didn't get this far by giving up."

The afternoon slipped away as we continued our research, building a profile of a woman who'd spent decades positioning herself to reclaim what she believed was her family's stolen inheritance. By the time the sun set, we had a clear picture of our adversary, and it wasn't encouraging.

"She's smart, connected, and patient," summarized Malakai. "She's been planning this for years, maybe decades. And now that she suspects there's gold in your building, she won't stop."

"So, what do we do?"

"We stay alert, we stay together, and we make sure the Lucky Break team knows what they're dealing with." He moved to the window, checking the street with automatic precision. "And we accept that this is going to get worse before it gets better."

The weight of that realization settled over me like a blanket. Twenty-four hours ago, my biggest worry had been budget overruns on the renovation. Now I was hiding gold in a gun safe and researching a woman who appeared willing to kill for what she believed was hers by right.

"I need a drink," I said.

"Good idea. And dinner. You haven't eaten since this morning."

He was right. As focused as I'd been on researching Margaret Quinn, I'd forgotten about food. My stomach growled as if to emphasize the point. "What do you have?"

"The basics. I'm not much of a cook, but I can manage steak, pasta, and salad."

I watched him move around his spartan kitchen, noting the way he checked the windows every few minutes, how he positioned himself so he could see both entrances to the living area. Even in his own home, he never relaxed.

"You know," I said, accepting a glass of wine, "most

people would be terrified by everything that's happened. The break-ins, the armed intruders, the discovery that their family building is being targeted by professional criminals."

"Most people?"

"I should be terrified, and in a way I am. But I'm..." I searched for the right word. "Exhilarated? Like I'm living instead of just existing."

He paused in his seasoning of the steak, studying my face. "Adrenaline can be addictive."

"Is that what this is?"

"Part of it. Your body's been flooded with stress hormones for days. Fight or flight response. It can make everything feel more intense."

"Including this?" I gestured between us.

"Especially this," he said, his voice raw.

The air felt charged with possibility. Enough that I set down my wineglass and moved closer to him, drawn by the heat in his eyes and the memory of how perfectly we'd fit together the night before.

"Amelia," he said, his voice rough with warning.

"What?"

"If we do this again, if we keep going down this path, there's no taking it back. You'll be part of my world, with all the dangers that entails."

"I'm already part of your world," I said, reaching up

to touch his face. "And from what I can see, any danger we're facing is down to my side of things, not yours."

He caught my hand, pressing it against his cheek. "I want you to be sure."

"I am sure. About you, about this, about whatever comes next." I stepped closer, eliminating the last bit of space between us. "I'm done being careful, Mal. I'm done playing it safe."

ELEVEN

MALAKAI

Amelia's declaration was all the invitation I needed. I crushed my mouth to hers, tasting defiance and surrender all at once. She kissed me back with the same hunger, teeth scraping, tongue claiming, a wildness that left my pulse hammering.

The edge of the dining table bit into her hips as I caged her in, my fingers tangling in her hair, tugging until she gasped. That sound made my cock throb, demanding I take her right there.

When I lifted her onto the tabletop, she wrapped her legs around me, grinding against my hardness with no trace of hesitation. My hands slid under her t-shirt, greedy for skin, dragging the fabric up until she tore it over her head herself. She was as quick to unhook her bra and toss it to the side, leaving me free to fill my palms with the swell of her breasts, the heat of her bare skin making me curse.

"Are you sure?" I rasped, my forehead pressed to hers, my hands already roaming lower.

"I've never been surer of anything in my life," she whispered, fumbling with my belt, her fingers trembling.

That was it. No more restraint. No more holding back. No more denying myself or her.

I claimed her with my mouth, trailing bites down her throat, across her breasts, circling a tight nipple until she moaned and arched for more. My tongue traced her ribs, her stomach, the faint quiver of muscles beneath.

She tugged at my hair, urging me down, and after helping her to lie back on the table, I gave her what she wanted. Tasting her, lapping at her slick folds until she cried out my name, thighs trembling against my shoulders.

By the time I stood and thrust into her, she was wet and desperate, clutching me so tightly I almost lost control on the first stroke. She cried out, her words inarticulate at first, then becoming clearer as passion built.

"Need you," she gasped, her nails scoring my back. "Need you so much."

The words hit me like a physical blow because they echoed exactly what I was feeling. Not just want, but need. She'd become necessary to me in ways that should have terrified me.

As her hips rocked to meet mine with reckless need, the table shook beneath us, every thrust deep, relentless, her heels digging into my spine as if to anchor me inside her.

I drove into her with a rhythm that bordered on savage, yet every kiss, every touch carried the weight of something profound. She was mine, and I was hers, and in that moment nothing outside these walls existed.

"Don't stop," she whispered, her voice breaking. "Please never stop."

The table became our altar, every movement a prayer, every gasp a promise. We fucked like we were burning alive, every cry and stroke stoking the fire higher until she shattered beneath me, clenching around me so hard it dragged me over the edge with her.

When I carried her over to the couch, we collapsed slick with sweat and spent, her hair stuck damp against my chest, and our clothes lay strewn like debris from a storm. The air was thick with sex and something more dangerous.

"That was..." she managed, voice hoarse.

"Incredible," I finished, still feeling the aftershocks.

She laughed, breathless, giddy. "I was going to say life-changing."

I pulled her closer, breathing in her scent. "That too."

She was quiet for a long moment, tracing lazy patterns on my chest. When she spoke, her voice was thoughtful, not rushed.

"Can I tell you something?"

"Anything."

"I've been thinking about what you said about trust. About how caring makes you vulnerable." She lifted her head to look at me. "I've spent my whole adult life avoiding that vulnerability. Choosing safe men, safe relationships, safe everything."

"And now?"

"Now I'm lying naked with a man whose real name I didn't know a week ago, planning to fight for a building that's brought me nothing but trouble." She smiled, but there was something profound in her eyes. "And I've never felt more like myself."

My chest tightened. "Amelia—"

"Relax, I won't get mushy on you," she said, before pausing. "Maybe that's a lie. All I'm trying to say is that this matters. You matter. More than I expected, more than I planned for."

I pecked her before giving her space. "What do you see when you look at me?"

"Someone worth trusting. Someone worth the risk." Her voice dropped to a whisper. "Someone I could build a life with, if he wanted that too."

There was no missing it had taken balls for her to say that, her breathing shallow, her expression haunted, as if waiting to be rejected.

The words hit me like a physical blow. I should have panicked. I should have thought about all the reasons this was impossible. Instead, I felt something settle deep in my chest, something that felt like coming home.

"Amelia—"

"I know it's ridiculous," she rushed out. "I know we haven't known each other long enough. But I can't help how I feel."

I tipped her chin up, forcing her to meet my eyes. "What do you feel?"

"Safe. Alive. Like I've been waiting my whole life for you to walk into that warehouse." She took a shaky breath. "Like maybe this is what life is supposed to feel like."

I kissed her then, soft and thorough, tasting hope and possibility on her lips. "I feel it too," I admitted against her mouth. "Whatever this is between us, I feel it too."

As we lay plastered together, her fingers traced lazy circles over my chest. On seeing how relaxed she was, I knew for certain she had no recollection of what she'd said in the heat of passion.

And given I wasn't sure how I felt about it, I wasn't bringing it up. Not when we were in the middle of a dangerous situation. If I were to get her through this safely, then I needed to focus, not lose myself in my attraction to her.

We dozed together wrapped in a throw blanket, and for a little while I let myself imagine this was our normal life. That we were just a couple in lust, love, or something in between, planning a future together, without the shadow of danger hanging over us.

The illusion shattered when a sharp beep from my security system cut through the peaceful silence.

"What's that?" asked Amelia alert in a heartbeat.

"Motion sensor," I said, already reaching for my jeans. "It might be nothing, but I still want to check it out."

I pulled on my jeans but didn't bother with a shirt, moving to the bank of monitors to see what had triggered the alarm. The screen showed movement near the back corner of my property. It could have been an animal, could have been the wind moving branches. Either way, I was checking it out.

"Stay here," I said, grabbing a gun from the safe. "I'll be right back."

"Mal, I don't like this." Amelia was already reaching for her clothes, that nervous energy I'd learned to trust radiating from her.

"It's doubtless nothing, but I won't be able to relax until I check it out."

I smashed my lips down on hers for a second before heading for the gun safe. With a gun stuffed down the back of my jeans to leave my hands free, I crept down the stairs leading to the garage, my bare feet silent on the treads. The cool night air hit my skin as I slipped outside, every sense on high alert.

The yard was quiet, shadows cast by security lights creating pools of illumination across the hardscrabble landscape. I moved with precision along the perimeter, checking the areas where the motion sensor might have been triggered.

I was examining the back corner of the property when I felt a sharp sting in my neck. My hand shot up, fingers closing around the dart before it could deliver its full payload. But even having yanked it out, enough of the tranquilizer had entered my bloodstream for my vision to blur and my legs falter.

I tried reaching for my gun, but my hand wouldn't obey the command. I was still trying when the world tilted sideways and my knees hit the gravel beside the garage.

Through the haze descending over my consciousness, I heard voices. Footsteps. The sound of my front door being forced open.

"Where's Mal?" Amelia's voice was sharp with fear. "What have you done with him? I want to see your badge numbers now!"

I tried to call out to warn her, but my vocal cords weren't responding. All I could do was watch as two figures in tactical gear emerged from my house, one of them carrying Amelia's limp form.

Of the two men, the larger was thick around the middle, his tactical vest straining over his gut. The other had a noticeable limp, favoring his left leg as he helped maneuver Amelia toward a vehicle I could only see the back of.

She was doing her best to fight them, I could tell, but whatever they'd hit her with had left her body limp even as her eyes remained conscious and terrified. Our eyes met for a moment across the distance, and I saw the trust there. The absolute faith that I would find her.

The tranquilizer pulled me under before I could see them drive away.

. . .

I came to still sprawled on the gravel with no idea how long I'd been out. Long enough that I was shivering like a wet dog, my mouth tasted of copper, and my head pounded like someone had used it for batting practice.

The dart still lay beside me where I'd dropped it. While I waited for my rage to burn through the drug haze, I couldn't erase the image of Amelia's terrified eyes looking back at me as they took her.

The woman I... dammit, I loved her. It was just a shame it had taken her being kidnapped for me to admit it to myself. And now she was in the hands of professional criminals, and I'd watched like a drugged animal while they carried her away, leaving me paralyzed in the dirt.

I stumbled back into the house, noting the splintered door frame and the chaos in my living area. They'd ripped the place to bits, doubtless looking for the gold. However, the gun safe had been left untouched, but only because they'd have needed heavy equipment to breach that.

My phone was where I'd left it, and I speed-dialed Chase while pulling on boots and a shirt.

"Mal? What's wrong?"

"They took her," I said, my voice still slurred but cracking with panic. "Christ, Chase, they took Amelia, and I couldn't do a damned thing. I couldn't move, couldn't even fucking speak. I just watched them carry her away."

"What? When? How many—"

"Two men, tactical gear, fake police patches, I think. They hit me with a tranquilizer dart about twenty minutes ago." Conscious I was still slurring my words, I stretched my mouth wide and then lubricated it as best I could before I continued. "I need the team here now. Ethan, Tyler, Daemon, Cole. Whoever's available. We're going to get her back."

"I'm on it. Are you okay to function?"

"I'll have to be." I said, already moving to the equipment lockers at the back of the garage, my hands shaking as I pulled out gear I hadn't used in three years. Every second felt like a lifetime. She was counting on me, and I'd already failed her once tonight. "Chase, what's the status of those vehicles?"

"That's why I was about to call you. The second vehicle left the freight company about an hour ago, but it hasn't come back. The tracking device shows it to be stationary now, about fifteen miles north of town."

"The mine?"

"Yeah, it is. I'll confirm the freight company is empty and meet you at your place in ten."

I hung up and continued gathering equipment. Night vision goggles, tactical vest, enough firepower to take on a small army, although my preference was to avoid it.

Nothing would bring the authorities to my doorstep quicker than us going all with all guns blazing. And yet I'd risk blowing my cover if it meant rescuing Amelia. I'd disappear into the night and reinvent myself in some far-flung location if it meant saving her.

The familiar routine of preparing for a mission helped focus my mind, pushing away the fear that threatened to consume me.

Amelia was counting on me. I wouldn't let her down.

Ethan arrived first, followed soon after by Tyler and Daemon, who pulled up together, with Cole's gleaming black Escalade coming up the rear. The sight of my teammates, my family, gathering in my garage filled me with a fierce satisfaction.

"What do we know?" Ethan asked, all business.

"Two suspects, both male. One heavy-set, one with a limp. Professional equipment but not professional behavior. They left me alive and didn't secure the scene." I spread a tattered map of the area on my workbench. "Chase tracked a vehicle to the Lucky Strike mine."

"That's Margaret Quinn's property," said Tyler. "The old mine's been abandoned for decades, but there are still some buildings up there. When we were kids, we used to dare each other to visit there at night."

"Defensible position," Cole observed, letting me know he was also familiar with the setup. "They chose it for a reason."

Chase answered my call before it had even had time to ring. "What's the status at the freight company?" I asked, not bothering with pleasantries.

"Empty. I wanted to wait long enough to be sure. Wherever they took her, it's not here."

"Which makes the mine our primary target." I pointed to the map. "It's isolated, they control access, and they can see anyone coming for miles."

"How many are we dealing with?" asked Daemon, his tone relaxed.

It hadn't taken me long after meeting him to realize there was more to Daemon than his laid-back attitude let on. From captain of the school wrestling team, he'd apparently moved onto illegal street fights, resulting in a spell behind bars. That was how he'd ended up working for Ethan.

"Not sure. We saw twelve at the warehouse, but some of those might have been hired muscle for the search. The core group could be smaller."

"Or larger," said Cole, his pessimism on full display.

I agreed with him on that front. "Margaret Quinn's

had decades to plan this. She might have called in favors we don't know about."

I steadied my voice, pushing down the terror that threatened to overwhelm me. The thought of what they might do to Amelia, what condition we'd find her in... I couldn't let the team see how close I was to losing it.

"I won't lie to you," I said. "This could go sideways fast. We're going in against an unknown number of hostiles in a defensible position, and we need to get Amelia out alive. If anyone wants to walk away, now's the time."

"Like hell," Ethan said. "She's part of the team now, and that makes her being taken our problem, not just yours." This surprised me given his hard and fast rule about the team not fraternizing with clients, which was ironic considering he'd met his wife on the job.

Tyler nodded. "Mal, you pulled me out of a bottle three years ago when my life was falling apart. We've got this."

Daemon's usual smirk was gone, showing me just how scary he'd have appeared to anyone facing off against him in a street fight. "Besides, these assholes made it personal when they tampered with the basement wall and came close to taking us out. Nobody terrorizes people on our watch."

Cole concentrated on checking his weapon. "Been looking for a good fight. Getting soft in my old age."

In looking around the team, something settled in my chest. These men weren't just my coworkers anymore. They were my brothers. And they understood Amelia wasn't just a client in trouble. She was family.

"Alright," I said, pulling up satellite images on my tablet. "Let's talk about how we're going to bring her home."

The Lucky Strike mine sat in a narrow valley about fifteen miles north of Coogan's Break, accessible by a single winding road that would leave us exposed for the last two miles. The main mine entrance was flanked by a jumble of wooden buildings that had doubtless housed offices and equipment storage back in the day.

"I'd forgotten how much like a movie set it looked," said Tyler, studying the aerial photos. "Like an old West ghost town."

"That's the problem," I said. "Multiple buildings give them plenty of places to hide, and we won't know which one she's in until we're already committed."

"What about thermal imaging?" Chase suggested.

"Thermal scopes will pick up heat signatures, but these old buildings are just as likely to give us false readings. We're going in somewhat blind."

Cole traced the access road with his finger. "They'll have lookouts posted here and here. No way to approach without being seen."

"Unless we skip the front door altogether," suggested Daemon. "Do we know what the backcountry's like? It's gotta be easier to negotiate than my last date."

I pulled up topographical maps, studying the ridge that ran behind the mine property. "Steep, but manageable. We could approach from the east, come down over the ridge."

"That's rough country in the dark," said Tyler. "My dad used to hunt up there, and it's ankle-breaking terrain." His follow-up grimace told of his having first-hand knowledge.

"Better than walking into a kill zone," I replied. "We go in quiet, identify where they're holding her, and then extract with minimal engagement."

"And if they won't let her go without a fight?" Tyler asked.

I met his gaze without flinching. "Then we remind them why that's a bad idea."

We spent another twenty minutes planning

approach routes and contingencies, but there was nothing left to do but gear up and move out. As I strapped on body armor for the first time in three years and undertook a final of my weapons, the familiar weight settled around me like a second skin.

As I took in the others, I realized these men weren't just risking their lives for a job or even for me. They were here because somewhere along the way, we'd stopped being coworkers and become family. The sort of family that didn't ask questions when one of their own needed help.

I'd sworn I was done with this life. Done with the violence, the split-second decisions that could mean life or death. But watching the woman I loved disappear into the night had reminded me who I was underneath the construction worker facade.

I was a predator. And someone had just taken my mate.

"Let's go hunting," I said.

The moment I realized they had Amelia, something cold and familiar slid into place. The part of me I'd tried to bury, tried to leave behind with Malcolm Tremaine, rose to the surface like oil in water.

I checked my weapons with the methodical precision of my former life, and for the first time in three years, I felt completely in control. It should have been reassuring.

Instead, it terrified me.

This was who I used to be. Who I'd sworn never to be again. But they had Amelia, and I would become the devil himself to get her back.

The question was: would she still want me when she saw what I was capable of?

The drive to the staging area took twenty-five minutes, following back roads that would keep us out of sight of the primary access route. We parked the vehicles in a grove of trees about two miles from the mine, with Chase soon joining us. After securing the vehicles, we continued on foot, using night vision equipment and flashlights with red filters to navigate the rough terrain.

The ridge approach was every bit as challenging as the maps had suggested, but we made good time despite the conditions. These men had all faced worse in one form or another, and they moved with the quiet efficiency of a team that trusted each other.

As we crested the ridge and got our first look at the Lucky Strike mine, I understood why Margaret Quinn's team had chosen this place. The hodgepodge of wooden buildings spread across the valley floor looked like something out of a Western movie. The only difference was that these buildings were the real deal, all that was left of the Campbell empire.

"Geez, Tyler wasn't joking. It's like a theme park," mumbled Chase. "Two-bit tourist trap."

Lights were visible in three of the buildings, and we could see at least two guards patrolling between them. The thermal scope picked up heat signatures in what looked like the old assay office, but I couldn't tell how many people were inside.

"That's where they'll have her," I said, pointing to the building. "Central location, excellent sight lines, multiple exit routes."

"Guards are sloppy," Cole observed. "Routine patrol, no communication checks. Whoever they are, they aren't professionals."

"I'm wondering if they aren't family members," I said, remembering something I'd read about Margaret's family in some of those newspaper articles. "More fool them if they think this will be easy money."

I studied the layout through my scope, but something wasn't adding up. Too many blind spots, too many places they could hold Amelia that we couldn't see from here. We could take the guards, breach the buildings, and still come up empty if they'd stashed her somewhere else.

There had to be a better way.

"Change of plans," I said, lowering my scope. "I'm going in alone."

"Like hell," Ethan growled. "We didn't come this far to watch you commit suicide."

"Not suicide. Strategy." I kept my voice calm, working through the tactical implications. "They'll be expecting me to come to the rescue, right? But they won't be expecting you lot. So, I'll give them what they're expecting, but on my terms."

"Explain," said Cole, his tone suggesting he wasn't dismissing the idea entirely.

"I walk in, hands up, looking desperate and panicked. Make them think I'm trading myself for Amelia. While they're focused on me, you move into position."

"That's a hell of a risk," said Tyler.

"Less risk than a frontal assault when we don't know where she is." I checked my watch. "Give me thirty minutes to get into position. If I'm not back with her by then, you come in hard."

"What if they just shoot you on sight?" asked Ethan.

"They won't. I'm worth more to them alive. They'll want to know what I know, what I've discovered about their operation."

The plan was risky, but it was our best shot. We spent another few minutes working out communication protocols and fallback positions, then I started making my way down the ridge alone.

The approach to the compound was easier than expected, with the amateur guards so predictable as to be easily avoided. I'd even relaxed a bit when I snuck around the corner of a small shack and straight into a guy guard who wasn't as sloppy. Despite not wanting to kick up a stink, I was left with no option but to deal with him, using skills long abandoned.

After I'd slammed my fist into his jaw, I'd expected him to hit the dirt as had been my experience in the past. But this guy obviously hadn't got that script. Instead, he shrugged off my punch as if it were nothing and did his best to return the favor.

With our position hidden from the team on the hillside, I knew it came down to him or me coming out victorious. And with Amelia's safety in the mix, there wasn't a chance I was letting this thug take me out.

Adrenaline shot through me as Malcolm Tremaine emerged fully formed from where I'd buried him, and I went from human to feral in a heartbeat. After that, the guy never stood a chance.

Unfortunately, when I lowered his unconscious form to the ground behind a stack of old mining equipment, I knew I was every bit as bloody as he was. It was something that saw me wrench his jacket off him and wipe myself down as best I could.

Body still spiked with cortisol, I had to fight to calm

the fuck down in order to deliver my lines with authenticity. As ready as I'd ever be, I stepped into the light, hands raised, and called out to the building.

Time to give them exactly what they thought they wanted.

TWELVE

AMELIA

The first thing I noticed was the rumble of an engine that had had a lot of work, followed by the musty smell of old fabric pressed against my face. My head felt like it was stuffed with cotton, and my body moved as if I were underwater, or treacle.

Memory came flooding back in fragments. The police smashing in Mal's front door and my demanding badge numbers. After that, everything was a blur.

I was in a vehicle, lying on what felt like a bench seat, covered by a scratchy blanket that smelled of motor oil and cigarettes. My hands were zip-tied behind my back, the plastic cutting into my wrists.

"She's waking up," a voice said from the front of the

vehicle. Deep, male, with a slight accent I couldn't place, but wherever he was from, it wasn't California.

"About time," another voice replied. "Thought you might have killed her with that thing."

Panic clawed up my throat, making it hard to breathe. I tried to sit up, my vision still blurry from whatever they'd hit me with. The blanket slipped, allowing me to see the back of two heads in the front seats, both wearing caps pulled low on their heads.

"I want to see your badge numbers!" I said, my voice hoarse but defiant. "I'm an American citizen, and I demand to know what agency you're with!"

The driver glanced in the rearview mirror, and I caught a glimpse of dark eyes above a black mask. "Stupid bitch thinks we're with that lot," he said with what sounded like amusement.

"Hah, yeah, sure we are," the passenger replied. "She can think whatever the fuck she likes."

ICE. Immigration and Customs Enforcement. They had to be, their refusal to identify themselves, their masks, their being more out of shape than I was. My heart hammered against my ribs as I thought about my dark hair, eye color and olive complexion that people often mistook for something else. "There's been a mistake," I said, fighting to keep my voice steady. "I was born in Sacramento. I have documentation—"

"Shut up," the passenger said, but not unkindly. "You'll find out soon enough what this is about."

The vehicle slowed and turned, gravel crunching under the tires. From the little I could see out of the side window, I knew we were climbing into the hills, the lack of rumble from the wheels pointing to us being on a dirt road. Maybe I knew where I was headed after all, and it wasn't the local ICE office, although even that wasn't a given these days.

"Where are you taking me?" I demanded. "I have rights. I demand to speak to a lawyer!"

"Bitch doesn't shut up, does she?" the driver muttered.

The truck came to a stop, and both of the front doors opened in tandem. Cool night air flooded in, carrying a waft of pine and something else. Old wood, rust, decay. The door beside me opened, and hands reached in to pull me upright.

"Come on, princess," the man said. He was the larger of the two I'd seen at Malakai's house, the buckles on his tactical vest being put to the test. "Time to go."

They hauled me out of the vehicle, my legs unsteady beneath me. When the blanket slipped, one of them grabbed it and wrapped it tight around me, leaving me fighting for air.

As busy as I'd been, hyperventilating, I was inside

before I could take in my surroundings, not that I thought it would help me know where I was. And if I didn't know where I was, then what chance was there that Malakai could find me?

The sob ripped out of me, followed by another and another. Much as I wanted to stop, I was powerless to do so.

"Aw, fuck, you can give that a rest too," said the guy with the limp. "It isn't gonna help you none."

Despite a concerted effort, I was still snuffling away when they dragged me inside a building that looked to be on its last legs, and dumped me without ceremony on the floor. With my hands zip-tied behind my back, I couldn't break my fall. The impact drove the air from my lungs, leaving me gasping and helpless.

Sobbing was now the least of my worries, with me more concerned about catching my breath, something I only managed with grit and determination. I would not let these low-life scum belittle me, even scanning my surroundings as a means of distraction.

"What is this place?" I asked, more confused than scared now. The last time I saw something like this was at a ghost town I'd visited with my parents when I was a kid. Of course, back then, the dilapidated state of the buildings we'd explored was down to artifice, and not a century of neglect.

"Welcome to the Lucky Strike mine," the driver

said. He was thinner than his partner, with a noticeable limp that made him favor his left leg. "Your family's old stomping grounds."

My family. Understanding hit me like a physical blow. "Margaret Quinn."

"Smart girl," said the large man, nudging me to one side with his foot. "Though I guess you'd have to be, being an architect and all."

It took me longer than it should have to put the pieces together. My knowing who was behind my abduction meant I wasn't meant to escape. This was a one-way trip as far as my captors were concerned.

The door of the main building opened, and four more men entered. Unlike my captors, these weren't wearing tactical gear. Just jeans and jackets, with bandanas or ski masks covering their faces. They looked like weekend warriors playing dress-up, and somehow that made them more frightening than the professional gear had.

"About time," one of them said. "We were thinking you'd gotten lost."

"Shut it, Derek," my driver replied. "Everything went according to plan." He then limped around me, his gaze speculative as the floorboards creaked under our combined weight.

"Oh, my lord, this place is a death trap," I said, looking up at the sagging roof beams.

"Funny you should say that," said an unfamiliar voice.

I craned my neck around to see a smaller man stepping out of the shadows. Thin and with nervous eyes above his mask, I recognized him, with my skin crawling in response.

"You!?" I said. "You're from the planning department. What are you doing here? Is this why you tried to warn me off the renovation?"

"Guilty as charged," he said with a mock bow. "Though I prefer to think of it as offering friendly advice. A pity you ignored it. Well, that and a very generous offer for that dump you seem smitten with."

"If he comes looking for her, this building will be the first place he'll check," interrupted one of the new arrivals. "We should move her now."

"Yeah, I'm not sure how long that mongrel with the stupid mustache will be out cold. He was bigger than I thought," said the wannabe warrior who'd helped kidnap me.

The weasel pulled out an expensive-looking phone and hit a speed dial number. "It's done. We have her." He paused, listening. "Yes, ma'am. The mine, just like you said... No, he's unconscious but alive... I understand. Whatever it takes."

He hung up and looked at the others. "Aunt

Margaret wants this finished tonight. And don't forget, it needs to look like an accident."

Fear spiked through me as I realized what they intended. "Wait, you don't have to do this. Whatever Margaret Quinn is paying you, I can match it. Double it."

"This isn't about money, honey," the weasel said. "This is about family. About setting the record straight after more than a century of lies."

They produced heavy-duty rope from somewhere; the kind used for marine applications or construction. There was so much of it I felt like a damsel in a Western movie, minus the railroad tracks.

"Please," I said, as they began winding the surrounding rope. "You don't understand. He'll come looking for me."

"We're counting on it," the weasel replied.

They trussed me up with professional efficiency, binding my arms to my sides and my ankles together. When they lifted me, I felt helpless, like a sack of grain being moved from place to place.

"Where are you taking me?" I asked as they carried me outside.

"Somewhere safe," said the limping man, giving into girly laughter before carrying on. "At least until the coyotes find you."

They carried me across the compound toward what looked like a black hole in the hillside. The entrance to the mine itself. As we got closer, I could see wooden supports framing the opening, old timbers that looked like they might have been there since the original mining operation.

"You can't put me in there," I said, panic rising in my voice. "What if it collapses? What if—"

My concern was met with yet more laughter, with it devoid of all humor.

The tunnel was narrow but tall enough for them to walk upright while carrying me. Their footsteps echoed off stone walls, and the air grew stagnant as they carried me ever deeper underground.

Battery-powered lanterns had been placed every twenty feet or so, creating pools of light connected by stretches of darkness. However, the space was nowhere near bright enough to bring me any measure of comfort.

As uncomfortable was when they dragged me along the rough wall at one point, the exposed rock snagged my clothes and any exposed skin. If I didn't know better, I'd think they were avoiding something on the ground, like abandoned machinery.

About fifty yards in, they stopped and dumped me on the tunnel floor. The dirt floor beneath me was cold and damp, and I could hear water dripping somewhere in the darkness ahead.

"Comfortable?" the weasel asked with false solicitude.

"Go to hell," I replied.

"We'll be back once your boyfriend arrives," he said. "Try not to go anywhere." He followed this useless instruction up by stuffing a bundled-up cloth in my mouth.

As busy as I was panicking to breathe, it took me a moment to realize they were leaving, and smashing the lanterns as they passed. As their footsteps weakened, so did any remaining light, leaving me in the dark and cold, desperate to gain control of my rising panic.

I lay there shivering, fighting waves of claustrophobia as the weight of the mountain pressed down around me. As time crept by, I made a promise to myself that if I got out of this alive, I'd level the warehouse myself. No amount of family history is worth dying for.

Now and then, I'd test the ropes, desperate to free myself. While I'd loosened a knot or two, it would take far longer than I had to free myself. My fingertips were already raw from wrestling with the knots.

It was while struggling with the bonds that I felt something hard pressing into my back. At first I thought it might be a rock, but when I worked my fingers around to touch it, I felt smooth glass.

A bottle. Small, maybe three inches long and an

inch around, with what felt like a cork stopper. It was also heavier than its size would suggest, and when I shook it, I could hear something shifting inside. Something that made a soft sound, like sand or...

Gold flakes, or dust, or even pickers!

My heart hammered as I realized what I'd found. This had to be from the original mining operation, a sample bottle that some long-dead prospector had left behind. Perhaps even Jeremiah. It was this last thought that had me clutching it until my knuckles hurt, the glass soon warm in my hand.

Time seemed to slow, and no amount of shifting helped my body ache any less from lying on the rough floor. Every drip of water, every settling stone made my breath catch. Every sound became a threat creeping closer. Were those footsteps? Voices? Or just the mountain settling around me?

Then I heard it. A grunt, distant but unmistakable, came from out near the buildings.

I struggled to roll over, peering down the tunnel toward the entrance. From where I lay, I had a perfect view of the compound, with the tunnel mouth facing the main building like looking down a telescope.

My eyes having adjusted to the dark, I was just able to make out several men moving between the buildings. It had to be Malakai and the others. They'd come for me. Or rather, he'd come for me.

I was even thinking it would be okay when security floodlights blazed to life, turning night into day. I then watched in horror as a single figure approached the front of the main building, hands raised in the universal gesture of surrender.

Even at this distance, I'd know that silhouette anywhere.

"No," I sobbed into my gag, when all I wanted to do was scream at him to defend himself. What was he doing? In the short time I'd known him, I'd never seen him surrender to anything or anyone. He was my rock.

But Malakai didn't pause, didn't hesitate. Rather, he walked straight up to the front of the building, making no attempt to hide his approach. He was within striking distance of the front door when he called out something I couldn't quite hear from this distance.

All I knew was that there wasn't a chance of his being able to negotiate with this lot. They'd already proved themselves to be the lowest of the low. They were the sort to Taser first and ask questions later.

On seeing the door open, and figures moving inside, this is what I expected to happen. Instead, the weasel appeared at the entrance, gesturing for Malakai to come forward. My heart hammered as I watched the man I loved walk into what had to be a trap.

When the door shut on them, my heart was in my

mouth as I waited for all hell to break loose. It made no sense for a man with Mal's skills to hand himself over like that.

Minutes ticked by with nothing happening. No gunfire, no shouting, just the occasional glimpse of movement through the windows. What were they talking about in there? What kind of deal was Malakai trying to make? Was he still alive?

This last thought had me sobbing against my gag, tears running down my face in an endless stream.

It felt like an eternity before the door reopened, and Malakai and the weasel walked out, my heart soaring in response, although now I was confused. I'd expected the other men to join them, with my experience to date telling me the Quinn family preferred to hunt in packs.

That wasn't the case tonight, with just the Mal and the weasel making straight for the tunnel entrance.

"Your boyfriend's here!" yelled the weasel when they arrived at the mouth of the tunnel. He pulled a high-powered flashlight from his belt. "Time for the big reveal."

He shone the light down the tunnel, the beam reaching all the way to where I lay. I squinted against the brightness, my hands instinctively protecting the glass bottle hidden behind me.

"She's there if you want her," laughed the weasel. "Safe and sound, just like I promised."

"Let me see if she's okay," came Malakai's voice, tight with controlled emotion.

"You can see her fine from there," the weasel replied. "Now, about the terms we discussed..."

The light clicked off, plunging me back into darkness as I listened to their voices moving away from the entrance. They were negotiating. Malakai had surrendered himself to bargain for my freedom.

The wait seemed endless. Then I heard new footsteps enter the tunnel. Purposeful, coming straight toward me without hesitation, although whoever it was soon stumbled to a halt.

"Hang on, Lia, I can't see fuck-all in this place."

"Malakai," I mumbled against my gag, making it as loud as I could.

Light appeared again, but this time it was the green glow of night vision goggles. However, I was confused when, rather than step forward; Malakai let out a string of profanities. He must have come close to tripping over whatever it was the men had avoided earlier.

"Amelia? Hold tight. It's okay. I'm coming. Whatever you do, don't move."

Seconds after this useless instruction, he reached

my side, pulled the gag from my mouth and awkwardly gathered me into his arms.

"I'm here," he said, his voice breaking. "Hell's teeth, Amelia, when I walked into that building and you weren't there, I thought I was too late. I've never been so fucking scared in my life."

"I knew you'd come," I whispered against his neck. "But what did you do? How did you get them to let you come down here?"

His hands shook as he worked on the ropes. "I told them I'd trade myself for you. Made them think I was surrendering because I was desperate and panicked." He paused in cutting through a stubborn knot. "What they didn't know was that the team was in position outside."

And he hadn't gone inside unprepared. He'd been wired for sound, letting the other men know they weren't outnumbered after all.

"Are you hurt?" His voice was rough with emotion as the last rope fell away. "Did they—"

"I'm okay," I said. "I'm okay now that you're here."

We held each other in that dark tunnel, both of us shaking. I could feel his heart hammering against his chest, matching the frantic rhythm of mine.

"What's the plan?" I whispered.

"In about ten seconds, those idiots up there are going to realize they've been had. The team's moving into position now." He helped me to my feet, testing my stability. "Can you walk?"

"I think so, although I might need some help." This was backed up when I finally stood and was hit with a vicious case of pins and needles. While waiting for that to abate, I looked toward the tunnel entrance, where voices were growing louder and more agitated. "Mal, they're coming back."

"Right on schedule. When I give the signal, we move toward the entrance. I want you to stay behind me and try to step right where I step."

The voices outside were getting louder and sounded more and more panicked.

"The others?" I said, "Are they okay?"

"Everyone will be fine. Come on, let's get out of here," said Malakai as he started toward the tunnel entrance, being careful to keep me tucked in behind him.

When we reached the mouth of the tunnel, I saw the Lucky Break crew moving with military precision through the compound. Tyler and Daemon were securing the perimeter while Chase and Cole covered them.

Ethan had taken a position outside the main building, with us soon joining him.

"How's it going?" asked Mal, his gaze never still as he swept the open area for any sign of life.

"Those assholes took off when they realized they were outgunned," said Ethan with a laugh. "Fucking Meal-Team-Six wannabes."

The floodlights were still on, but the place was quiet. Too quiet. Of the vehicles that had been parked near the buildings earlier, only one remained.

"They got away?" I asked, part of me annoyed at this development. I'd happily kick that little weasel in the shins for the hell he'd put me through.

"For now. They said they had the mine set to blow, and I couldn't take the risk that they weren't bluffing. We had to choose between letting them go and getting you to safety." After scooping me up as if I weighed nothing, he carried me to where Tyler and Daemon were now waiting. "I chose you."

According to the others, Mal and Chase were still checking the abandoned buildings for any stragglers. Of Cole there wasn't any sign, and yet I was sure I'd seen him earlier.

"How badly are you hurt?" asked Mal, setting me down on the tailgate of the remaining truck.

"I'm okay. Scared, sore, but okay." Only then did I hold up the glass bottle I'd been clutching. "Look what I found."

Malakai's eyes widened as he took in the small bottle filled with what looked like gold dust. "Where did you get this?"

"I was lying on it in the tunnel. Some relative of mine or Margaret's must have dropped it forever ago." I looked around at the concerned faces of the men who'd risked their lives to save me. "I can't believe you all came after me. Do you have any idea how dangerous that was?"

"About as dangerous as sitting around doing nothing while the woman Mal cares about was in the hands of criminals," said Chase as he rounded the corner of the nearest building.

Ethan soon backed up this sentiment from his brother. "Yeah, we'd never have heard the end of it if we hadn't helped."

Rather than respond to this lame attempt at humor, the anger that had been building since my rescue boiled over. "Are you crazy? You could have been killed. All of you! And for what? That stupid warehouse of mine, thirty thousand dollars worth of gold, and whatever this dust is worth?!"

Malakai was quiet for a moment, studying the bottle in the glare of the floods. Then he looked at me with those dark eyes that had become so precious to me.

"Are you sure this and the thirty grand is all of it?" he murmured.

"What do you mean?"

"I mean, if Margaret Quinn's family has been

obsessing over this mine for generations, if they've spent decades destroying your family's properties looking for gold, do you think they'd go to all that trouble for such a small prize?"

Not to be left out, Daemon then put his two cents' worth in. "It won't have been cheap buying up all those properties, even if there was a return after she developed the sites." His theory was sound enough that it got a positive response from all the others.

I stared at them and then at Mal. "Do you think there's more?"

"I think," said Malakai, "that what we found in the basement at your place might just be the tip of the iceberg. And I think Margaret Quinn knows it."

What Malakai said made sense. With the warehouse the only Donovan property not yet bought and leveled, any missing gold had to be there.

I was still giving thought to other potential hiding places back at the warehouse when Cole ambled out of the dark, his expression unreadable. "I just checked, and the guy whose truck this is said it'd be okay if we borrowed it."

He followed this up by opening the driver's door, climbing in, and fiddling with something under the dash. A moment later and the engine roared to life. "Come on, you lot, I'm not getting any younger."

I was next into the cab, with Mal joining me. All

the others climbed into the bed of the truck for the return to wherever they'd left their own vehicles.

As we pulled away, I took in the abandoned mine compound and the wooden buildings that had housed generations of dreams and disappointments. Whatever we were mixed up in, it wasn't over. Not even close.

The drive felt endless. I stayed pressed against Malakai's solid warmth, my hand fisted in his shirt like he might disappear if I let go. Every bump in the road made me startle, my body still convinced danger lurked around every corner.

"It's over," murmured Mal, against my hair. "You're safe now."

Safe, the word felt foreign after hours of terror. But with his arm around me and his familiar scent tickling my nose, I believed it might be true.

The man I loved was alive and whole, and by the time we reached the vehicles, I knew it without a doubt. Crazy that it had taken hours in the dark for me to come to terms with this. And when I thought he'd been hurt, it felt as if that little weasel had reached inside my chest and crushed my heart.

THIRTEEN

MALAKAI

The ride back to where we'd left our vehicles was subdued, with Amelia pressed close against my side in Cole's borrowed truck. I could feel the tension radiating from her body, the way she startled at every unexpected sound. The adrenaline was wearing off, leaving her crashed and shaky.

I'd come so close to losing her, I was just as shaken. The terror I'd felt when I thought she might be gone forever had crystalized something I'd been trying not to acknowledge. She wasn't just someone I cared about anymore. She was everything. The center of my world. My mate, in every way that mattered.

"You okay?" I whispered, pulling her even tighter.

"Getting there," she murmured against my shoulder. "Just processing everything."

By the time we reached our vehicles, dawn was lightening the eastern sky. The team dispersed with promises to meet later, everyone needing sleep and time to decompress from the night's events.

The drive to my house took twenty minutes, during which I checked the mirrors as often as any social media star and took an indirect route. Old habits from my previous life, but after tonight, I wasn't taking any chances.

Once we were inside my garage, I went through my security checklist twice. Motion sensors, camera feeds, perimeter alarms. Everything was functioning as it was designed to.

But I added a few extra precautions, setting up improvised early warning systems that would alert me to any approach. Determined not to be caught unawares again, I even included a couple of nasty surprises for the unwary.

"Mal," whispered Amelia from where she stood watching me work. "You're scaring me a little."

I looked up from the tripwire I was adjusting. "Sorry. It's just—after tonight, I need to know we're as safe as I can make us."

"Are we safe?"

The honest answer was that safety wasn't assured

so long as Margaret Quinn was free and obsessed with recovering what she saw as her family's stolen legacy. But Amelia had been through enough for one night.

"For now," I said, pulling her into my arms, holding her close. "We need to stay alert until Margaret and her remaining crew are caught. But you're here, you're safe, and that's what matters right now."

"How long do you think—" she started.

"Let's not think about timelines tonight," I interrupted gently. "Let's just focus on the fact that you're okay."

She nodded against my chest, and I felt some of the tension leave her body. The heavy conversation could wait. Right now, she needed to feel secure.

The shock was setting in, her body processing the trauma of being kidnapped and held in that mine tunnel. There wasn't a chance I was telling her about the pit a mere ten feet from where they'd dumped her.

The last thing I did when we got inside was to screw the door shut, vowing to replace all of it with something stronger the first chance I got.

Upstairs, Amelia stood in the middle of the living room, still wearing her torn clothes, and I could tell when the reality of what had almost happened hit her like a physical blow. Her legs gave out, and she sat on the couch, shivering, although not from cold.

"I thought I was going to die in that tunnel," she whispered. "I thought I'd never see you again."

I was beside her in an instant, pulling her against my chest, holding her like I never wanted to let her go, which I didn't. The alarm system could wait.

"Come on, sweet thing," I said. "Let's get you warmed up."

I led her into my bathroom, a utilitarian space that had one luxury. The deep soaking tub I'd installed when I'd renovated the place had once graced a high-end hotel in San Francisco. I started the water running, adjusting the temperature until it was just shy of scalding.

It was when turning on the faucets that I'd noticed how bloody my hands still were. A quick look in the mirror above the vanity confirmed I hadn't cleaned up as well as I'd thought. The only thing in my favor was that Amelia hadn't run screaming for the hills when faced with the bloody evidence of my dark past.

Not wanting to risk her seeing the state of me, I grabbed a facecloth and wiped my face clean before pumping soap onto my hands and scrubbing at them, the sting of the cuts grounding me.

"What happened to your hands?" she asked from right behind me, the words not much above a whisper.

I'd looked down at the split skin, the evidence of what I'd had to become to reach her. "There was a guard. Between me and the building where I thought they were holding you."

"You had to..." She hadn't finished the question.

"I had to take him out. It was the only way to get close enough to execute the surrender plan."

I turned to face her, letting her see the truth in my eyes. "For a few minutes tonight, I wasn't Mal Torres anymore. I was Malcolm Tremaine again."

She'd stepped closer, taking my damaged hands in hers. "And that scares you."

"Terrifies me. The ease with which I slipped back into that mindset, the muscle memory, the cold calculation." I met her gaze. "I swore I'd never be that person again."

"But you did it to save me."

"I would have done worse to save you. That's what scares me most."

She'd kissed my knuckles, broken skin and all. "I'm not afraid of what you had to become. I'm grateful for it."

"'Turn around," I mumbled, relieved to still have her trust.

She complied without question, trusting me despite everything she'd been through. I worked at the zipper of her jacket, then the buttons of her shirt, treating her as if she were made of spun glass. Her clothes were dirty from the mine, torn in places from her struggles against the ropes.

"Those bastards," I muttered under my breath as I saw the rope burns on her wrists, and her bleeding fingernails.

"I'm okay," she said, but her voice was small.

"No, you're not. But you will be."

I helped her step into the hot water, watching as she sank into it with a yelp of pain that soon changed to a soft sigh of relief. With the heat easing the tension in her muscles, some color returned to her pale cheeks.

"Room for two?" I asked.

She looked up at me with those dark eyes that had become my salvation. "I don't want to be alone right now."

I wasted no time stripping and sliding into the water behind her, pulling her back against my chest. For a long time, we just sat there in the steaming water, her head resting on my shoulder as I ran gentle hands over her arms and shoulders.

"I thought they were ICE agents at first," she said after a time, her voice still racked with fear.

"What?"

"When they first grabbed me. They had the tactical gear, but they were so out of shape, so unprofessional. It reminded me of some of the videos I've seen online.

You know, where they're desperate to fill quotas and standards have slipped."

I tightened my arms around her. "Sheesh, Amelia."

"As soon as I saw the mine, I knew it wasn't true. But for those first few minutes in the truck..." She shuddered. "I was terrified they were going to deport me somewhere I'd never been, just because of how I looked."

The rage that swept through me stole my breath. If I ever got my hands on them again...

"Hey," murmured Amelia, turning in my arms. "Where did you go?"

"Just thinking about what I'd like to do to the bastards who hurt you."

"They didn't hurt me. Not really. And you saved me." She squeezed my arm. "You came for me, just like I knew you would."

"I was terrified. When I rushed into that building. That wasn't tactical. That was pure panic. I was expecting to find you..." My voice broke. "I've seen what people do to hostages when they're desperate. The thought of them hurting you came close to destroying me." I shook my head at my own stupidity. "I could have gotten us all killed."

"But you didn't. And I'm here, and you're here, and we're both alive."

She kissed me then. Soft at first, almost

hesitant. But the sweetness burned away in seconds, replaced by heat, by hunger. Relief turned primal, and we were clinging to each other as if the world outside had never existed. We'd come so close to losing everything, and were now desperate to prove we were alive, that we were still here, still ours.

"I need you," she whispered against my mouth, her fingers threading into my hair, tugging, pulling me ever closer.

"Are you sure? After everything—"

"Because of everything," she cut me off, her voice fierce and shaking. "I need to feel alive. I need to feel us."

I growled low in my throat, crashing my lips back to hers. My hands claimed her curves, tracing the swell of her breasts, the softness of her hips, the sweet dip of her waist.

She pressed against me, her body lush and warm, every inch of her begging to be claimed. My scars caught beneath her fingertips as she mapped my chest and shoulders, but instead of pulling back, she lingered, kissed me harder, like she wanted to own every broken piece of me.

My cock was already hard, aching, jutting against her stomach as I slid my fingers between her folds, parting her slick heat, stroking her swollen bud. Her head fell back, lips parted, the sound of her breathless moan filling the tiled room.

"Fuck, I want you so bad," I groaned, teasing her pearl with slow circles until her hips bucked.

"I want you," she gasped, rocking against my hand. "Only you."

I couldn't wait another second, and the bath wouldn't give me the purchase I'd need. "Come on, Lia, I'm getting waterlogged."

Despite her protests, I had us both out of the bath and dried off in record time. Soon after she was spread across my California king like the most delicious repast ever, with me a starving man.

But eating could wait, because right now I wanted to fill her. I nudged myself into her slick depths, savoring every inch as her sheath stretched around my cock. She was so tight, so hot, clenching down on me until I had to grit my teeth not to lose it right there.

"God, you feel perfect," I groaned, burying myself to the hilt.

She clung to me, arms and legs wrapped tight, her nails scoring across my shoulders as I moved. Each thrust drove me deeper, harder, her soft curves bouncing against the solid muscle of my chest. The bed shook beneath us as I drove myself into her relentlessly, her cries growing louder, more desperate.

Reaching between us, I found her pearl again,

rubbing it with my thumb as I pounded into her, and she shattered. Body tightening, thighs trembling, her core clenching around my cock as she screamed my name. Sobbed that she loved me.

The sight of her coming undone pushed me over the edge. I drove into her with ragged, desperate thrusts, spilling deep inside her as I groaned her name and my own words of love against her neck, shaking with the force of it.

We stayed locked together long after the last shudders passed, sweaty and trembling, our hearts hammering as one. Morning light poured through the bedroom window, gilding her flushed skin, her swollen lips; her curves still quivering from my touch.

"We should get some sleep," she murmured, though her hand smoothed over my chest, fingers pausing on a scar like she never wanted to let go.

"You might be right," I agreed, kissing her hair, still buried in the scent and warmth of her. "But not yet. I can't let go of you yet."

"Then don't," she whispered without preamble. "Never let go."

My bed had never felt more like home than it did that morning, with Amelia curled against my side as the sun streamed through the bulletproof windows. We dozed in fits and starts, both of us too wired for anything else, but content to be together and safe.

I traced lazy patterns on her shoulder, my fingers following the curve of her collarbone, when the weight of what I'd been keeping from her became too much to bear.

"Amelia," I mumbled, my voice rougher than I intended.

"Hmm?" She shifted against me, tilting her head to look up with those dark eyes that undid me every time.

"There's something else I need to tell you," I said after she'd settled against me. "About what happened in that tunnel. I want to protect you, but it's better you know ..."

"Tell me," she whispered. "I can handle it."

I struggled with the words, running my hand through her hair. How do you tell someone you love how close they'd been to death?

"When I found you in that tunnel," I began, then stopped. Started again. "When I was trying to get to you, I came close to taking a fall."

"Ah, I wondered. Was that what you were cursing about?"

I peppered her shoulder with kisses while thinking about how to break the news.

"I'm so sorry, Mal. I didn't think to warn you about the pile of equipment. The men who carried me in scraped me against the wall to avoid it."

I stilled, wondering whether I should let her know

the truth of it. Then I decided I had no choice but to tell her. I'd want to know if I were in her position. And what if she took it into her head to go looking for more abandoned bottles of gold? If anything happened to her, I'd never forgive myself.

"It wasn't old equipment they were avoiding, Lia. There was an open shaft. Taking up most of the tunnel floor." I felt her breathing change. "Just... a black hole dropping God knows how deep into the mountain."

She was quiet for a long moment, processing. When she spoke, her voice was barely a whisper. "That's why they were so careful about where they stepped. Why they avoided that section of the tunnel when they were carrying me."

"Yeah. They knew it was there. But what they hadn't expected was for me to have night-vision goggles. Without those..." The rage I'd been suppressing since the rescue threatened to surface again. "Those creeps deliberately dumped you on the other side of it, hoping..."

"That in trying to save me, you'd die." She followed this up with a sob, her grip on my biceps even tighter.

"Maybe. Although I think it was more that they hoped you'd loosen those knots and try to escape before I turned up."

She lifted her head to meet my eyes. "You think they wanted it to look like an accident."

"I know they did. Margaret Quinn's been planning this for forty years. The crazy old bat wouldn't want anything traceable back to her." I dragged her into a tighter embrace. "Christ, Amelia. When I think about how close I came to losing you, it just destroys me."

"But you didn't lose me." Her fingers traced one of the scars across my ribs. "You found me. You saved me."

She was quiet again, and I could see her working through the full implications of what I'd told her. The shaft, the deliberate placement, how easily it could have gone wrong.

"I'm glad you told me," she said finally. "I needed to know. All of it."

"I wasn't sure if I should. You'd been through enough."

"Hey." She shifted up to look at me properly. "We're partners now, remember? In everything. That means no protecting me from the truth, even when it's ugly."

I nodded, some of the tension I'd been carrying since the rescue finally easing. "Partners."

"Besides," she added with a slight smile that didn't quite hide the shadows in her eyes, "I was already planning to have nightmares about that tunnel. Might as well have all the facts for my subconscious to work with."

As my lips claimed hers, I marveled at her strength.

Another woman might have fallen apart learning how close she'd come to death. Amelia was already figuring out how to process it and move forward.

"No more secrets," I promised against her hair.

"No more secrets," she agreed, settling back against my chest. We lay there in the growing quiet, both of us processing everything we'd survived.

When she spoke again, her voice was barely a whisper. "Mal, there's something I need you to know too..."

"What is it?" I asked gently.

"When I watched you surrender yourself to save me... when that door closed behind you and I couldn't see what was happening..." Her voice caught. "I realized something important."

"Tell me, beautiful."

"I realized that what I feel for you isn't just gratitude or attraction." She paused. "It's everything."

"Amelia, when I thought I might lose you tonight..." I stopped, trying to find words for what I'd felt in those moments. "I've lost people before. But the thought of losing you wasn't just pain. It was the end of everything I wanted for my future."

She stilled against me.

"I love you," I said, the words steady now instead of rushed. I'd been fighting the knowledge for days, but tonight had stripped away all my defenses. "Not because we survived something traumatic together, but because you changed everything. You make me want to be the man I used to be, the man you deserve."

Her eyes filled with tears. "Mal..."

"I know it's fast. I know we're in the middle of chaos. But some things you just know, and I know I want to spend whatever life I have left making sure you never doubt how much you mean to me."

Life was too tenuous for me to hold back and perhaps miss the opportunity. The lucky escapes we'd had tonight had proved that beyond doubt.

She settled back against my chest, her hand over my heart. "Tomorrow, we'll face whatever comes next. Tonight, I just want to be here with you."

"Tomorrow," I agreed, though I knew that when morning came, there would be words that needed saying. Feelings that had crystallized in the darkness of that mine, in the terror of almost losing each other.

But she was right. Tonight was for holding each other, for being grateful we both survived, for letting the foundation of something deeper settle between us.

The declarations could wait for daylight. They'd be no less true for the waiting.

FOURTEEN

MALAKAI

It was early afternoon before we'd finished telling and showing our love for each other, although I suspected we weren't done yet.

On meeting up with the others at the warehouse, I'd half-expected to find the building vandalized or damaged in some new way. However, it stood as we'd left it, solid and defiant against the blue sky. Definitely in our favor was so many of the Quinn clan lying low.

"Thank God," Amelia breathed when we pulled up outside the warehouse.

Her expression told me everything. "You thought about tearing it down yourself, didn't you?"

She was quiet for a moment. "When I was lying in that tunnel, terrified I was going to die, I thought about a lot of things. And yes, for a moment, I considered whether any building was worth risking the lives of people I care about." She made eye contact before adding, "The people I love."

She then followed this up with a cheesy grin that matched my own.

"But you didn't. Give up, that is."

"No. Not when I realized that's what Margaret Quinn wants. For me to give up, to walk away from my family's legacy. I'll be damned if I let that miserable old crone win. Not after what she's put us through."

The team was already assembled in the basement, with Ethan and Tyler examining the north wall where we'd found the first cache of gold. Daemon was helping with equipment setup and, for once, in no rush to get anywhere else.

"Do you reckon another woman has seen the error of her ways?" said Tyler, tipping his head toward our resident Romeo.

"Hey, at least someone wants me for more than just my good looks," Daemon called out, overhearing. "Even if it's just to carry heavy crap."

"How's the security looking?" I asked.

"A truckload better," said Ethan. "Between what you installed earlier and what Chase is adding now, we'll know if a mouse so much as farts."

"Good. Because you know they're not done with us."

Cole appeared from the shadows near the main staircase, moving with a silent grace that told me there was more to him than he let on.

"I've got us a headquarters," he said without preamble. "Upstairs over Murphy's cobbler shop, right across the road from here. Old Murphy doesn't ask questions, and he's gone fishing for the week."

"What kind of setup?" asked Chase, not bothering to look up from the motion sensor pad he was installing under the stair tread.

"Two large windows facing the street, perfect sight lines to the warehouse. External staircase at the back so we can come and go without being seen. Space for all our gear."

"Perfect," I said, my arm settling on Amelia's shoulders. "How long until everything's in place?"

"Give us a few hours," said Chase. "The surveillance gear should be operational by then."

"A few hours? Isn't that cutting it fine?" repeated Amelia, worry in her voice.

"Sure, it's tight, but we'll still be ready for them," I said, wrapping my arms around her. "Even if the setup is only half-assed, we won't be caught off guard."

"What if they don't come tonight?" pressed Amelia.

"Then we'll be set up and waiting tomorrow," I said. "Either way, we're not backing down."

By that evening, our makeshift headquarters above the shoe repair shop looked like something out of my old life. Cole had gotten hold of a pair of trestle tables, which were now laden with monitors, comms equipment, and other surveillance gear of the type I thought it was better not to ask about.

"Geez, Cole," said Tyler, looking at the setup. "Where did you get all this stuff?"

"Don't ask questions you don't want answers to," replied Cole with a grin.

The view from the windows overlooking the street was perfect, just as our resident silver fox had promised. We could see the warehouse and all the street approaches.

With the improved sensor array and cameras, we had complete coverage of the building's interior and perimeter, including the alleyway at the back. There wasn't any chance of the Quinn gang taking us unawares.

Never again would I allow that to happen, to suffer the gut-wrenching worry of having someone I loved at the mercy of those without scruples.

"Now we wait," I said, settling into one of the lawn

chairs Cole had provided, with Amelia sitting in a matching model next to me.

"With luck, this might even beat my usual Saturday night," said Daemon, with a dirty grin.

We didn't have to wait long.

It was just after midnight when we first noticed movement on the bank of screens. Lurching to my feet, I watched the feeds over Chase's shoulders, able to see two trucks turn into the alleyway down the side of the warehouse.

I then followed them from one monitor screen to the next until they pulled up next to the rear entrance. A glance was enough to confirm they were the same vehicles as last time.

"I honestly didn't think they'd turn up tonight," I mumbled, gripping Amelia's hand when she joined me. "Greedy bastards thought it would take us a day or two to get our shit together."

The team gathered around, and we watched four men climb out of each truck and approach the large back door. They were moving with more care than on earlier occasions, as if they'd learned from their previous failures.

"Same crew?" asked Chase.

"Seems to be from the look of things. I recognize the guy with the limp," I said. "But they're carrying some crates that they didn't have last time." I leaned forward to get a better look at the monitor. Holy mother. I recognized the logo from a box I'd seen at the mine. "That's fucking dynamite."

"How much?" asked Ethan, abandoning his spot next to the lace curtains that concealed him from anyone looking up. When he joined us looking over his brother's shoulder, the air was thick with testosterone.

"More than enough to level the building," I said, my tone one of mild confusion. But then it came to me. "Damn it, they're not planning to steal the gold this time. They want to destroy everything and buy the rubble."

"Like hell," said Amelia, her jaw set at a mutinous angle.

We then watched as the intruders opened the back door using a forged keycard, doubtless courtesy of Howard Pruitt. We were then able to monitor their progress through the building thanks to the motion sensors and CCTV.

Thanks to our hidden cameras, we could see where they placed their charges, their movements and the locations concise, as if rehearsed. This was in marked contrast to their performance the night before. It did, however, confirm that their actions weren't a random act of vandalism, but a calculated demolition plan.

"There," Daemon pointed to one of the monitors.

"Basement level. They're setting charges at the base of the main load-bearing wall."

"And there, and there," said Tyler, tapping the tops of a couple of other monitors. "There'll be nothing left standing if they take those out."

Then something went wrong.

A bright flash lit up the basement level, followed by an explosion that rattled the windows of our headquarters on the other side of the street. Dust and debris filled the camera feed, obscuring our view.

"Premature detonation," said Chase, flicking through the various screens. "Looks like one of the charges went off early."

"No bloody surprises there," I said. "The crate I saw at the mine looked to be damp. Any idiot knows if you don't keep it dry, it's a freaking accident waiting to happen. I'm just glad it didn't take out any of the walls, or else we'd be dealing with rubble and cadaver dogs."

When the dust cleared, we could see chaos in the basement. The large guy who'd helped kidnap Amelia was lying motionless under a pile of rubble, while the others scrambled around in pure panic.

"Broke his legs, looks like," I said, studying the feed. "They'll have to carry him out, because they sure as fuck can't leave him there."

And that's when our opportunity presented itself.

I knew it'd take at least four guys to carry that lump

up to street level, and for that they'd need a stretcher of some kind. The worst-case scenario was they'd have to use something like a tarp. And as luck would have it, there was already one in the basement.

As four of the men stood around their injured comrade, they argued about the best way to move him. In the confusion and dust, with several of the basement lights now knocked out, visibility was poor.

"This is our chance," I said, already rummaging through the pile of gear next to the door. "Tyler, Ethan, Daemon, you're with me."

"At last, some excitement," said Daemon with a chuckle. "It'll make a change from having drinks chucked in my face."

"What?" gasped Amelia, and for a second I thought she was shocked about Daemon's dating game, but then she continued. "You can't just waltz in there. Not with all that dodgy dynamite, and those thugs on edge."

"Lia, stop worrying. We're dressed enough like them to get away with it. All we have to do is take them out after they've dumped their mate in the back of one of the trucks. In all the chaos, the three left in the basement won't realize we're ring-ins until it's too late."

"That's insane," she said.

"No, that's brilliant," Cole corrected. "Hide in plain sight. They'll never expect it."

I'd already studied their appearance from our

surveillance footage and knew their dark clothing, ski masks, and baseball caps would be easy enough to replicate. It took us less than a minute to pull on caps and cobble together makeshift masks.

When we were dressed, I looked around the team, taking particular note of Daemon. He matched me in height, something I often forgot given his boxer's build. Where I had the shoulders of a linebacker, he was all compact muscle and coiled energy. The sort of build that could move fast and hit hard.

"Headsets," said Cole, handing out communications equipment. ""These are encrypted so they can't monitor our comms."

"What about us?" asked Amelia.

"You stay here with Cole and Chase," I said, my tone telling her to obey. "Monitor the situation, and call for backup if needed."

"Mal—"

I kissed her hard and fast to stop her pleas in their tracks. "I'll be back. We all will."

The takedown went smoother than I'd dared hope, although we held back rather than rush in. To avoid being stuck with the dead weight of the guy with the broken legs, we waited until they'd manhandled him into the tray of one of the trucks.

By the time they'd managed that, they were sweating, swearing and dead on their feet, making our task of overpowering them a piece of cake. What they also hadn't expected was to be joining their downed comrade in the back of the truck.

Thanks to the industrial nature of the cable ties used to secure them, we knew they weren't going anywhere until we said so. And judicious use of gaffer tape meant there wasn't a chance of them yelling for help.

In the confusion and poor lighting, the three who'd stayed in the basement never questioned our appearance when we returned to help them. With the element of surprise in our favor, it was easy enough to take them down and tie them up.

"Basement secured," I reported through my headset. "There are seven suspects in custody, and one for the paramedics."

"Copy that," Cole's voice came back. "But we've got a problem. Another vehicle just pulled up out front."

Through the narrow basement windows, I could see additional figures approaching the building. But it wasn't additional muscle, with one an older woman, moving with the imperious bearing of someone used to being obeyed.

"Margaret Quinn," Tyler muttered.

"And the weasel from the planning department," added Daemon. "Driving her personal sedan."

"Perfect," I said. "Let's wrap this up."

Cole's voice crackled through the headset: "Amelia wants me to tell you she's got some choice words for that planning department asshole."

I had to bite back a laugh. Even in the middle of a tactical operation, my woman was making threats that could doubtless be heard three blocks away.

With the weasel using another forged swipe card to enter, we had to hustle to the point we were still stuffing the three captives under the stairs when Margaret Quinn inched her way down into the basement.

Despite her physical failings, she made up for it in what I thought was strength of will. The sort that could castrate a man with a single glare. Trailing behind her, in a vain hope of keeping his balls intact, was the weasel, his mannerisms a testament to how nervous he was.

He wasn't the only one who was nervous. What if the old lady realized it wasn't her young relatives she was dealing with? I'd just double-checked my mask was in place when Cole crackled to life through the comms unit.

"Amelia says to remember the old girl's blind as a bat. Something about cataracts when you first met her."

It was something that was confirmed when the old lady barely glanced in our direction, and with the weasel keeping his head down, I knew we were okay.

"What's taking so long? You should have leveled this place by now!" Margaret berated us. "I thought I taught you idiots how to handle explosives."

"Sorry, Aunt Margaret," I said in what I hoped was a passable imitation of one of the men we'd been eavesdropping on earlier. With any luck, her hearing would be as dodgy as her eyesight. "Derek got hurt when one of the charges went off early. They took him to the emergency room on account of his legs being messed up like they were."

"Useless," she spat. "Just like your father. Can't do anything right without someone holding your hand."

I watched with fascination as the woman revealed her true nature. This wasn't the respectable pillar of the community we'd researched. No, this was a bitter, vicious harridan who saw her own family as nothing more than tools to be used and discarded.

"Maybe if you paid us better, we'd be more motivated," yelled one of the real nephews from under the stairs.

Damn it, they didn't make gaffer tape like they used to.

"Pay you better?!" Margaret's voice rose to a shriek. "You ungrateful little shits! I've spent forty years planning this, forty years positioning myself to reclaim what's mine by right, and you want to negotiate?"

And there we had it. A recording of her incriminating herself.

"I think you'll find," I said, pulling off my mask, "that we're done negotiating."

The look of shock and rage on Margaret Quinn's face was worth every risk we'd taken. The weasel tried to run, but Daemon was ready for him, taking him down with a move he'd doubtless perfected when captain of the wrestling team.

"You," Margaret snarled, pointing a gnarled finger at me. "This is all your fault. If you'd minded your own business—"

"If I'd minded my own business, you'd have terrorized an innocent woman and stolen her family's legacy," I replied. "But that ends tonight."

Chase's voice came through the headset: "The cavalry's arriving. Three patrol cars, lights off. Guys we can trust not to be on the take. I can come deal with them if you like."

"That'd be great. Thanks," I replied, my stance relaxing. While my assumed identity was robust enough to fool most, my preference was to keep as low a profile as Howard Pruitt did when near his aunt.

Chase spoke again, although not as I'd expected. "And something else, Mal. That car Pruitt was driving.

Turns out Richard Pearson was Margaret's second husband. Guy divorced her in under a year, which is why she acts as if it never happened. The ex said that she was obsessed and unstable."

"So why is she being ferried around in his car?" I asked, curiosity getting the better of me.

"Turns out she's vindictive, too. Knowing he loved the car, she demanded it as part of the settlement and has kept it in perfect condition all these years, just to spite him."

Like her second husband, Margaret's nephews, once released, couldn't distance themselves fast enough, flying up the stairs and leaving Margaret behind.

"She's crazy," one of them told the arresting officer, tipping his head toward the basement stairs. "We just needed the money. We didn't know she was planning to blow up the entire building."

"Yeah, right," his cousin added. "She's been obsessed with this crap since we were kids. She never shut up about the gold, about how the Donovan's stole everything from us."

Margaret Quinn was the last to be brought up from the basement. Her perfect composure cracked. Gone was the elegant matron I'd encountered at the planning department with Amelia. This woman's face was twisted with rage and forty years of obsession.

"This isn't over!" she screamed as the officers led her across the road toward a patrol car. "That gold belongs to my family! Jeremiah Donovan was a thief and a murderer!"

When Amelia crossed the road and joined me out front of the warehouse, Margaret's fury only intensified, words pouring out in a torrent of decades-old rage.

"Your precious ancestor killed my great-great-grandfather, you conniving little gold digger! James Campbell found that gold fair and square, but Jeremiah wanted it all. He murdered James and stole everything. The gold, the mine claims, even this warehouse!"

When she followed this up by gesturing with abandon toward the building, it resulted in her smacking an officer square in the face with a handbag heavy enough to topple governments. But the demented shrew wasn't done by a long shot.

Her voice cracked as spittle flew from her lips. "James Campbell was a good man, and that bastard Jeremiah destroyed him! Just like his descendants have been destroying my family ever since!"

"The only thief was James Campbell," Amelia yelled back, surprising me with her boldness. "And you're just like him."

Margaret's face was now white with fury, and it

took three officers to wrestle her into the car. Even then we could see her ranting through the window, her face contorted with a rage that had consumed her entire life.

And then, with a farewell bleep of its siren, the patrol car left, with Margaret on her way to explain how she came to be in a building she didn't own at two in the morning. There was also the diatribe and footage Chase had recorded and sent to his contacts at the station.

"Do you think it's over?" Amelia asked as we watched the patrol car disappear around the corner at the end of the street.

"Yeah, I think it's over."

She threw herself into my arms, and I held her tight, breathing in her womanly essence and letting the reality reassert itself.

Now, all we needed to do was make sure the charges stuck, because something told me this would be troublesome as anything we'd faced tonight.

FIFTEEN

AMELIA

Any celebrations were short-lived.

I woke up late Monday morning feeling like we'd won something, curled against Malakai's hard chest as sunlight streamed through his bedroom windows. Margaret Quinn and her nephews were in custody, the cops had taken care of all the dynamite, and for the first time in weeks, I felt like I could breathe.

That feeling lasted until I checked my phone.

"Crap," I muttered, scrolling through a flurry of emails, with each more urgent than the last.

"What's wrong?" Malakai's voice was rough with sleep, but he was alert, with this being a habit from his previous life that I appreciated.

"The building permits. They've been suspended

pending a comprehensive review of historical accuracy and ownership documentation." I sat up, reading faster. "There's also a notice of environmental assessment required, and something about irregularities in the original property transfer dating back to 1855."

Malakai was already reaching for his own phone. "Let me guess. This all happened yesterday."

I had to scroll back through the emails before I could answer him. "Not yesterday. This morning, starting around seven. Margaret must have had these motions prepared in advance, ready to file the moment she was arrested." The sick feeling in my stomach was growing.

"There's more. The planning department is requiring new geological surveys, updated archaeological assessments, and..." I had to read this one twice. "Proof of legitimate ownership dating back to the original land grant."

"Fuck!" said Malakai, scrolling through something on his phone. "There are notifications from the alert I set on the court records system. Three different law firms have filed motions questioning the validity of your ownership. All representing interested historical parties."

I stared at him. "Three? How is that even possible?"

"Money talks. And Margaret Quinn's had forty years to build relationships." He was already getting out of bed, moving with that controlled urgency that meant he was shifting into tactical mode. "This isn't over, Amelia. Not by a long shot."

Malakai had only just put my coffee on the bedside table next to me and climbed back into bed with his own, when my phone rang. The number was blocked, but something told me I should answer. The same instinct also told me I should put the phone on speaker so Malakai could hear.

"Miss Donovan? This is Attorney James Morrison from Morrison, Kline & Associates. I represent the Campbell Historical Preservation Trust."

"The what?"

"I'm calling to inform you that my clients are prepared to make a generous offer to resolve the ownership dispute regarding the property known as the Donovan Warehouse."

"What ownership dispute?"

"Miss Donovan, I'm sure you know that recent historical research has uncovered significant questions regarding your family's claim to the property. The Campbell Trust has documentation suggesting that your ancestor, Jeremiah Donovan, may have got the property through fraudulent means."

"That's bullshit," I spat out, my professional demeanor in the trash.

"The courts will need to determine the validity of competing claims. Litigation of this nature can be expensive. And time-consuming. My clients are prepared to offer fair market value for the property, plus a substantial settlement to cover your renovation costs to date."

I looked at Malakai, who was shaking his head.

"How substantial?" I asked, though I already knew I wasn't interested.

"Four million dollars, Miss Donovan. Cash, with a thirty-day close."

Despite myself, I felt my breath catch. Four million dollars would solve every problem I'd ever had. It would pay off my business loans, give me financial security for life, and let me start over anywhere I wanted.

"I need time to think about it."

"Of course. However, I should mention that this offer expires in seventy-two hours. After that..." He let the threat hang. "Well, litigation can be quite unpleasant. And expensive."

After I hung up, Malakai put his coffee down and pulled me into his arms. "You're not considering it, are you?"

"It's four million dollars, Mal."

"It's blood money. They're trying to buy what they couldn't steal."

"But what if they're right?" The words tumbled out before I could stop them. "What if Jeremiah did cheat James Campbell? What if my whole family's been living a lie for over a century?"

Malakai's grip tightened. "Do you believe that?"

"I don't know what to believe anymore. All I know is that Margaret Quinn will kidnap and murder for this building. People don't do that unless they believe they're in the right."

For a second, Mal hugged me even tighter. "That, or they're out of their minds."

But I pulled away from him, got out of bed, and walked to the window that overlooked his backyard. "What if I fight this and lose everything? The legal fees alone could bankrupt me. And even if I win, it would tie me up in court for years. I'll never finish the renovation."

"So, Lia, let me get this straight. You're just going to give up?"

"I don't want to, but I have to be realistic."

"No, that's not true. You're letting them scare you off. And I get it. But this is what they want. They couldn't blow up your building, so now they're trying to blow up your will to fight."

I turned to face him. "And what if they succeed?

What if I lose everything fighting for a building that wasn't even mine to begin with?"

"Then we'll face it together."

The simple certainty in his voice broke me. Here was a man who'd already lost everything once, who'd had to rebuild his entire identity from scratch, and he would risk it all again for me.

"Mal..."

"I'm serious. Whatever happens, we're in this together. But I need you to ask yourself one question: Can you live with giving up?"

I closed my eyes against the morning light, thinking about my grandfather's stories, about the pride in his voice when he'd talked about Jeremiah Donovan. About the dreams I'd had for the warehouse, of bringing it back to life. About everything I'd already survived to get this far. "No," I whispered, feeling something steel inside me. "I can't give up. Not now."

"Then we fight," he said, getting out of bed and coming over to stand behind me.

I nodded, but the fear was still there, gnawing at me. "Mal, what if we're wrong about Jeremiah? What if he was—?"

"Hey," said Malakai, draping his arms over my shoulders and resting his chin atop my head as he looked at our reflection in the window. "You want to know what I see when I look at you? I see someone who's spent her entire career restoring things other people would tear down. Someone who sees beauty where others see decay. That instinct doesn't come from a family of thieves, Lia."

His words broke something loose in my chest, and the next thing I knew, I was crying. Not just about the building, but about everything. The fear, the doubt, the weight of carrying my family's legacy. Sunk as I was in despair, I was only just aware of him turning me around.

"I don't know who I am if I'm not a Donovan," I whispered against his chest.

"You're the woman who sees potential where others see problems. You're stubborn and brave and willing to fight for what matters."

He then squeezed me extra tight but for a second, as if to reinforce that what he was about to say was important. "You're the woman who made me want to stop running and start building something real. That's who you are, with or without that damned building."

I wasn't sure how it happened, but one moment Malakai was holding me together and the next I was pulling at him, tugging him back to bed like I might unravel if I didn't have his body to anchor me.

Only this man—this maddening, gorgeous man— could wipe my legal worries from my mind and have me feeling strong again. I needed that now more than ever.

And damned if he didn't have the body to do it.

In a move I'd never have contemplated in the past, I pushed him back onto the bed, my pulse racing at the sight of him sprawled there. Broad chest rising and falling, eyes burning with heat, his glorious erection straining for me.

My body trembled, but not with fear. Rather with hunger. God, he was beautiful. Beautiful and dangerous, and all mine.

But standing there, with heat creeping up my neck, I was having second thoughts, feeling foolish for having taken the lead.

I was still wavering when his voice broke through my self-consciousness. Low. Rough. Wicked. "I can lie here all morning and wait for you to decide, gorgeous. Or I can get up and convince you."

My pulse jumped in response to the promise in his voice, with a nervous laugh bubbling out of me. "Maybe...?"

He was on his feet in a heartbeat, his hands finding my hips. The contrast between his rough hands and the soft fabric of my oversized t-shirt when he lifted it over my head, sent a shiver rushing through me.

And then there was nothing between us, not even doubt. Especially not that. Skin to skin, flaws and truths bared alike. But instead of feeling exposed, I felt... powerful. Desired.

He eased me back onto the bed, his weight settling over me, and I could feel the thick press of him against my thigh. My body clenched in anticipation, already aching for him to fill me, to stretch me in the way only he could.

But he didn't rush. He trailed kisses down my chest, drawing my nipples between his lips, sucking until I cried out, pleasure knifing through me sharp and sweet. His tongue circled my buds, as though he had all the time in the world to worship me.

"Malakai..." My voice broke on his name, a plea and a prayer all at once, although what I was praying for I didn't know.

"Shh. Let me love you a little."

And he did. His mouth, his hands, every brush of his tongue, every slow stroke of his fingers was deliberate, grounding me. I arched beneath him, trembling as he teased me open, preparing me, coaxing me higher.

Then he hesitated. Reached for the nightstand. My breath caught when he pulled out a ring that had nothing to do with engagement, the soft hum when he turned in on betraying its true purpose.

"Is that...?" My voice was ragged, half disbelieving, half desperate.

He gave a sheepish grin. "You said you were open to new things. But if it's too soon…"

The thought of giving myself over to sensation, of drowning in it, sent a rush of heat through me. "I want it. Malakai, I need it."

Relief flickered across his face before hunger swallowed it whole. He briefly pressed the toy against my clit, with the vibration ripping a cry from me. My hips jerked, helpless, as pleasure roared to life under his control.

But this was nothing compared to the thrill after he'd clipped it around the base of his cock and slid inside me. The stretch was exquisite, every thrust driving the hum of the cock ring right where I needed it. My body clenched around him, my cries high and broken as he kissed my throat, my mouth, my breasts.

"God, Malakai. Yes, oh yes." The words tumbled out, wild and breathless, as the pleasure built inside me.

"Come for me, sweet Lia," he murmured against my skin, thrusts deep and sure.

The orgasm shattered me. Hot, violent, messy, it ripped through me until I was gasping and sobbing his name, my nails clawing down his back.

When the tremors eased, he collapsed beside me, pulling me into his arms. And in the silence afterward, wrapped in the scent and heat of him, I felt not broken but rebuilt. Desired. Chosen.

The next three days were a blur of lawyers, legal documents, and mounting pressure. Every day brought new challenges: environmental concerns that required expensive testing, archaeological surveys that could take months, questions about mineral rights and historical designations.

While Margaret Quinn might have been in jail, the network she'd spent forty years building was still executing her plans. Pre-arranged contingencies kicked in, favors were acted upon, and every permit I'd ever got was under scrutiny.

"She's got people everywhere," Cole told us during an emergency meeting at Malakai's house. "Planning department, city council, even some judges. Forty years of building relationships and digging dirt."

In response to my confusion, he added, "Digging up dirt on individuals, not mining."

By Thursday morning, I hadn't slept through the night in three days. Every email brought new legal threats, every phone call another demand for documentation I didn't have.

I was sitting at Malakai's kitchen table, surrounded

by papers and empty coffee cups, when he appeared beside me with a plate of scrambled eggs.

"Eat," he said without preamble.

"I'm not hungry."

"Eat anyway." He sat down across from me. "When's the last time you had a proper meal?"

I tried to remember, but I couldn't, which was so out of character as to unsettle me even more. "I don't know. Tuesday?"

"Amelia," he said, reaching across and closing my laptop. "The damned lawyers can wait twenty minutes." The set of his jaw told me that this wasn't open for discussion.

As I forced myself to eat, he moved to stand behind me. And as he massaged my shoulders, for the first time in days, I felt like I could breathe. This man was taking care of me in ways I hadn't known I needed.

"Why are you doing this?" I asked.

"Because you're mine to take care of," he said, like it was the most obvious thing in the world.

"But how? I can't ignore the lawyers forever," I said, forcing down the last mouthful.

He'd not elaborated when the motion sensors pinged, warning of movement outside. However, Malakai's being relaxed when putting my plate in the dishwasher told me he'd either been expecting someone, or knew who it was.

Leaving me to reopen my laptop, he thundered down the stairs and opened the front door, voices in the stairwell soon telling of the arrival of Daemon, Cole and Chase.

Only after there were coffees all around, did Mal and I bring the three men up to date with the latest legal challenges.

"Those assholes," said Cole. "Two can play at that game."

"What do you mean?" I asked.

"If Margaret's people can find problems with your paperwork, we can find problems with theirs," said the older man, although he offered no solutions of how.

"He's right, Lia. For starters, there's the Campbell Historical Trust. It was only founded six months ago."

"Six months?" said Chase, looking up from his phone. "That's awfully convenient timing, wouldn't you say?"

"Gets better," continued Malakai. "Guess who the primary beneficiary is?" Evidently not expecting an answer, he pressed on. "Rebecca Quinn-Morrison, Margaret's daughter. Lives in San Francisco, hadn't spoken to her mother in twenty years."

"At least not until there was money involved," muttered Cole.

"Family reconciliation through greed," I said. "How heartwarming."

Chase frowned. "What about the law firms coming after you?"

"Three of them, all part of the same umbrella corporation," said Malakai, "and that traces back to Margaret's real estate holdings through a shell company."

"She's been planning this for decades!" I slumped in my chair, my head hitting the dining table with a defeated bump.

"Which means she's invested everything in this," said Malakai with something akin to glee. "Money, reputation, relationships. She can't afford to lose."

"Neither can we," I said, dropping my head to the side so I could look at him.

For a moment, silence filled the room. We all understood the enormity of what we were facing. Decades of planning, unlimited resources, and a network of corruption that we were only beginning to uncover.

Then Daemon, who'd been sitting quietly as he often did, suddenly sat forward on the couch. "What if we're looking at this wrong?"

"What do you mean?" I asked, not bothering to lift my head from the table.

"We're trying to prove your family's innocent. What if we prove her family's claims are based on lies instead? If James Campbell was the actual thief, then Margaret's entire case falls apart."

It took me a second to sift through his suggestion, and then the idea hit me like a lightning bolt. "The mine. Margaret owns the Lucky Strike mine. If James Campbell was the victim, wouldn't Jeremiah Donovan have taken that, too?"

"When you put it like that, he doesn't sound like the victim to me," said Malakai, his words measured as though he was still working through the logistics. "What if Jeremiah wasn't the perpetrator after all?"

"We need to get back up there. To the Lucky Strike," I said. "From what I can remember, the main building was pretty much empty, but what if...?"

"Yeah, about that," said Chase, not giving me a chance to finish my thought. "After what happened at the warehouse, the police sealed the mine off while they dealt with any remaining dynamite."

In response to Cole clearing his throat, all eyes were soon on him. "I heard through the grapevine that the cops finished clearing the explosives yesterday. The place is technically still a crime scene, but..." He shrugged. "Security's pretty minimal."

His admission had me wondering, not for the first time, what circles he mixed in, with even Chase now giving him the side-eye.

. . .

That evening, after the team had left and Malakai and I were alone in his kitchen, he made us tea without asking. Somehow he'd figured out that I preferred it to coffee in the evening. Small observation, but it mattered.

As background to this, Malakai's phone buzzed with another message. This was the third one in half-an-hour, and each time, his expression had grown more tense.

"Everything alright?" I asked.

"Maybe. Hard to tell." Malakai looked up from his phone. "Some contacts from my previous life have been going dark. Radio silence where there shouldn't be any."

"Meaning?" I asked.

"Meaning something's spooked them. Could be unrelated to us, or..." He shrugged, but the casual gesture didn't hide his concern. "When people in my former line of work disappear, it usually means someone's rolling up the network."

"Rolling up?"

"Arrests. Federal investigations. The sort that makes everyone scatter to avoid getting caught in the net."

As if picking up on my nerves, he put his mug down, giving me his full attention.

"Are you okay?"

"Just processing everything, that's all."

"Regrets?"

I considered the question seriously. "About the warehouse? No. About dragging you into this mess and leaving you vulnerable? Yes."

He sat across from me, his expression serious. "Amelia, I want you to understand something. Nobody dragged me anywhere. I chose this. I'm choosing you, this situation, all of it."

"Why?"

"Because for the first time in three years, I have something worth choosing. Something worth fighting for that isn't just survival." He reached across the table, covering my hand with his. "You've changed everything for me."

I turned my hand palm up, lacing our fingers together. "You've changed everything for me, too."

We sat like that for a while, connected across the table, and I felt something solid form between us. Not just attraction or proximity or shared crisis, but something that could last.

Later that night, as I lay in bed with Mal, I was wondering about our planned visit to the mine. "What if we find nothing?" I asked, taking comfort in snuggling against the hard planes of his chest.

"Then we figure out Plan B," he said, smoothing my hair in measured strokes.

"And if there is no Plan B?"

"Can I tell you something?" he asked. He was then quiet for long enough that I thought he'd changed his mind. "I'm terrified."

I lifted my head to look at him. "You? Mr. Black Ops is terrified?"

"Not of Margaret Quinn. Or the legal battles." His hand traced patterns on my back. "I'm terrified of losing you. Of watching you give up on your dreams because I couldn't protect what matters to you."

"Mal—"

"I've lost everything before, Lia. My job, my identity, my whole life. But losing you would break me in ways I don't think I could come back from."

I kissed his chest, right over his heart. "Then it's a good thing you won't lose me, because I don't plan on getting lost."

As I lay against Malakai's chest, feeling his heartbeat steady beneath my cheek, the word *love* echoed in my mind. I couldn't believe I'd blurted out how I felt about him. Was I really falling for a man I'd known for little more than weeks?

The rational part of my brain—the part that had planned every detail of my career, that never made a move without careful consideration—was screaming warnings. This was too fast, too intense, too risky.

But the rest of me, the part that had been dormant for so long I'd forgotten it existed, was singing.

This didn't feel reckless. It felt like finally listening to my gut instead of ignoring it. Like my soul had been waiting for his, and now that they'd found each other, nothing else mattered.

I thought about the way he'd held me during the permit crisis, steady and unshakeable when my world was falling apart. The way he'd trusted me with pieces of his past, small fragments that painted a picture of a man who'd been hurt but wasn't broken. A man who understood that sometimes you had to risk everything to build something worth having.

This was it, I realized. This was what I'd been waiting for.

Not the safe, predictable love I'd always imagined. But this fierce, consuming thing that made me want to be braver, stronger, better than I'd ever been before.

I'd spent my whole life playing it safe, choosing the path of least resistance. But Malakai made me want to fight for something.

Made me want to take the biggest risk of all.

The risk of forever.

SIXTEEN

MALAKAI

The Lucky Strike mine looked different in daylight, less threatening but somehow even more tragic. The buildings that had seemed menacing in the dark were revealed as decaying remnants of a dead dream, weathered wood and rusted metal telling the story of hopes that had died with the gold rush.

"Hard to believe people lived up here," said Chase, surveying the ragtag of wooden structures scattered across the valley floor.

"Gold fever makes people do crazy things," I replied, thinking about Margaret Quinn's forty-year obsession. "Some people never recover from it."

The crime scene had been released late the day before, just as Cole had said. With most of the Quinn clan behind bars, and any others staying out of the way, we had the run of the place. This saw us splitting up to search, looking for anything that might shed light on what had happened between Jeremiah Donovan and James Campbell all those years ago.

With the main office close to collapse, there wasn't a chance I wanted Amelia anywhere near it. And the police tape crisscrossing the doorway told of their stripping it of dynamite and anything else not bolted down.

However, there were outbuildings and storage areas that Cole and Chase said appeared to have been ignored by the cops. Amelia and I were examining what looked like an old assay office when Daemon called out from nearby.

"Got something here!"

After some yelling back and forth, we joined him standing next to what appeared to be a root cellar, its wooden door hanging open to reveal stone steps leading down into darkness. Also alerted by the racket we'd kicked up were Cole and Chase, who'd abandoned their search of the outbuildings and joined us.

"How did the police miss this?" said Amelia as we joined Daemon.

"Door was covered by all this crap," he said, gesturing to the pile of canvas and dirt he looked to have just moved. "I was taking a leak when I noticed the ground felt spongy. Took some digging to find the actual entrance."

The cellar was well-preserved, the stone walls keeping the interior dry despite a century or more of neglect, although it was cramped after the five of us had inched our way down the narrow stone steps. And there, on a sturdy workbench, sat a wooden chest that looked like it hadn't been opened in years.

"Son of a mother fu...," muttered Cole, when we opened it and peered inside. "This lot is a treasure trove."

Papers. Lots of them. Journals, business correspondence, financial records, like a time capsule from the 1850s. But what caught our attention straight away was a letter sitting right on top, the quality paper folded to form an envelope of sorts.

Amelia reached for it, then stopped. "Should we be handling something this fragile without gloves?"

"We'll be careful," I said. "But we need to know what we're dealing with."

She lifted the folded paper and opened it out. Even from where I stood, I could see the handwriting deteriorated as if the writer had been under extreme stress.

In reading it aloud, Amelia was soon as stressed.

My conscience will no longer allow this deception. Jeremiah Donovan is an honest man, and I have wronged him beyond measure.

I have stolen the bulk of our partnership's gold and hidden it in various locations, intending to claim Jeremiah had taken it. I can no longer live with this burden of lies.

By the time this letter is read, I will have ended my own life, unable to face the shame of what I have done to a good man.

The letter was dated the day James Campbell had died from so-called natural causes.

"Suicide," mumbled Daemon. "The family must have covered it up."

"And built their entire legacy on the lie that followed," added Amelia, relief evident in her voice. "Margaret Quinn's ancestor wasn't a victim. He was a criminal."

"We need to get this lot somewhere safe," I said, looking at the chest full of historical documents. "This is evidence, but it's also fragile as hell."

"Shouldn't we photograph everything and leave it be?" said Amelia. "You know, to prove where we found it."

Cole shook his head, with Chase backing him up.

"The local force is a lot cleaner than it used to be," said the bounty hunter, "but it's still got a way to go. It's also better we take care of the documents than to leave them here for the Quinn family.

"Well, that, and photos can be dismissed as fakes these days," added Cole. "Too easy to doctor them. But you can't fake old paper and ink. The originals are the only proof that'll hold up if this goes to court."

"Right, so we take everything to keep it safe," said Amelia, understanding. "But we release just enough via email to put doubt on Margaret's claims. Let her wonder what else we might have found."

"That's it," said Cole with an approving nod. "She'll be too scared to push forward. If it comes out that James Campbell was actually the thief and a suicide? Her social standing, her historical society positions, her reputation. It all goes up in smoke. These documents are her worst nightmare."

"Smart," I said, pulling Amelia close and kissing the top of her head. "It's about time we controlled the narrative."

We closed the chest, with Chase and me then manhandling it up from the cellar. The thing was heavier than it looked, and it was no mean feat to maneuver it up the narrow stone steps and load it into my truck.

"We'll see you back at the house," I told the others while opening the passenger door for Amelia.

"I've got plans," said Daemon, with his, "Don't call if you need anything," giving me a fair idea of what his plans were. The guy was a man whore who seemed to attract women without trying. And that was why he was still single. Quality would always win out over quantity in my book.

The drive back to my place was quiet, both Amelia and I processing what we'd found. The confession letter alone was enough to destroy Margaret Quinn's entire case, but we needed to go through everything with a fine-tooth comb.

Chase helped me get the wooden chest up the stairs and into my living room, while Amelia headed for the shower. "Can't have people seeing me looking like I've been grave robbing," she said, before leaving us to it.

She was still in there when Cole arrived, with my concentration shot as I daydreamed about her current soapy state. It wasn't much better when she rejoined us wearing an all-access dress complete with flowing skirt. The damned woman would be the death of me.

And it wasn't just her who needed to be clean, something that saw the rest of us washing our hands and drying them twice to avoid damaging the fragile records. With that done, we spread the documents out across my large dining table, the five of us then examining them.

The evidence was overwhelming. James Campbell's journals detailed how much gold he'd siphoned from their joint operation. He'd been meticulous, recording every ounce stolen while keeping false books to show Jeremiah.

The correspondence revealed his plan to frame his partner, and the confession letter laid bare his guilt and desperation. The other thing that soon became apparent was that everything in the box dated back to a single year - 1856. James Campbell's last year of life.

"Damn it," said Cole, scratching his head. "That old bird has to know this lot's missing from the family archives, and there isn't a chance she'd want it being made public. With her family's reputation on the line, it might even be worth more to her than the gold itself."

"Listen to this," I said, reading from one of the journals. "JD grows suspicious of discrepancies in our accounts. When accusations are made, his word against mine won't help him. Have prepared additional evidence to ensure conviction."

"He was planning to frame Jeremiah all along," whispered Amelia. "That, that..."

However, it was the hand-drawn map we found at the bottom of the chest that made us all sit up and take notice.

"Check this out," I said, studying the detailed locations Campbell had marked. "Gold hidden all over the place, including..." I looked at Amelia with a grin. "The basement of a certain warehouse. And it's not where we found that lot the other night."

Her eyes widened. "There's more?"

"A truckload, by the look of things."

Armed with Campbell's map, we found what he'd described. A false wall that had survived over 150 years undetected. Behind it were several leather pouches filled with gold coins and nuggets, far more valuable than what we'd found earlier.

"Damn," Chase breathed as we laid out the contents. "This has to be worth a fortune."

"I can't believe James Campbell hid stolen gold here, right under Jeremiah's nose," said Amelia, her anger clear. "That bastard was planning to claim the warehouse after Jeremiah was hanged for his crimes."

After helping to repack the gold, Cole and Chase headed home, leaving Amelia and me alone in the transformed space.

"Come with me," she said, taking my hand. "There's something I want to show you."

She led me up to the top floor, to what had once been Jeremiah Donovan's private office, with me lugging the gold. Call me paranoid, but the Quinn family had shown themselves to be the lowest of the low, meaning there wasn't a chance I was leaving it unprotected.

Upstairs, Jeremiah's office felt almost secret, with west-facing windows allowing golden light to flood the space.

"This is where he would have planned everything," murmured Amelia, running her hand along the massive plan drawer unit that dominated one wall. "I had this piece refinished when I first started the project."

I should have been admiring the craftsmanship, but my focus was locked on her. On how the light gilded her curves, caught in her hair and softened the flush on her cheeks.

"Amelia," I said, my voice rough with need.

She turned, and whatever she saw in my eyes made her breath stutter. The adrenaline from our discovery, the relief of being proven right, the way she looked standing there like a goddess. It all hit me at once.

I crowded her back against the wall between the windows, my palms braced on either side of her head. "We did it," I growled, unable to stop myself. "We found the truth."

Her lips parted. "We did," she whispered, pressing her soft hands to my chest. "Together."

The word throbbed with promise. Together. Partners. Not just in this, but in everything.

I kissed her like I'd been starving for it, because I had. She answered with equal hunger, clutching my shirt in her fists, pulling me closer until her lush body molded against mine.

"Here?" I asked against her mouth, already desperate.

A moment later, she broke our kiss, and her gaze flicked to the wide, polished plan drawer unit. Her cheeks flushed darker, but her eyes burned. "There."

I wasn't waiting for her to change her mind. Instead, I lifted her, settling her onto the sun-warmed wood, the solid top the perfect foil for her curves. The sight of her sitting there breathless, skirts rucked up, legs spread to drag me between them, knocked the air from my lungs.

"Christ, Lia," I muttered, my hands sliding over the generous swell of her hips. "You don't know what you do to me."

Her thighs clamped around my waist, pulling me tighter. "Then show me," she whispered, her voice shaking with need.

I bunched her skirt higher, fingers finding the thin strip of lace clinging to her heat. She gasped as I brushed her sex, already damp, already aching for me. "You're so ready," I rasped, dragging the lace aside.

Her nails dug into my shoulders, urging me closer. "Then don't make me wait."

I fumbled with my belt, urgency making my movements rough, almost frantic. When my cock pressed against her slick folds, her heat had me close to losing it, and I had to force myself to pause. Just for a heartbeat, needing her to feel the choice.

"Lia ... once I start—"

"I won't want you to stop," she finished for me.

With a groan, I thrust into her, slow enough to feel every inch of her tight, wet sheath swallowing me. She cried out, head tipped back, nails scoring me, and the sound shattered the last of my control.

"Fuck, you feel incredible," I gasped, gripping her full hips, driving deeper.

She clung to me, moving with me, every lush curve cushioning and yielding under my hands, the office filled with the sound of us. Her breathless moans, my ragged curses, the creak of wood as I slammed into her harder, faster.

"More," she begged, her voice breaking. "Don't stop."

I kissed her throat, her jaw, drinking in every desperate sound. "Say my name," I demanded, my voice hoarse.

"Mal—oh God—Mal!"

Her climax tore through her, her body pulsing

around me in waves that dragged me under. With a last thrust, I spilled into her, groaning her name like a vow.

For a long moment we clung, trembling, the sunlight blazing around us. Only when I dragged in air again did I notice the soft click beneath my hand. A hidden mechanism triggered during our frenzied lovemaking.

A drawer had slid open from the side of the unit.

Amelia blinked at it, still flushed and tousled, hair falling wild around her face. "What the hell?"

"Looks like we triggered something," I said, fighting a grin as satisfaction burned through the haze. "And a hidden compartment."

Reluctant as I was to do so, I pulled free, my cock aching like it was ready for more, and to be honest, I wouldn't say no.

Still, there'd be plenty of time for that when we got home. Home? Yeah, I liked the sound of that. More than I had any right to.

Sliding down from the unit, Amelia tugged her clothes back into place, still trembling. Then she pulled the hidden drawer open, revealing papers inside, the handwriting different from what we'd found at the mine.

"Jeremiah's writing," she breathed, lifting out the first document with trembling fingers.

*My dear James. I hope this gesture will help
heal the growing rift between us. Sarah has
always admired the portrait of our wives, and I
thought having a copy made for your home
might remind us both of the friendship our
families once shared.*

As the letter fluttered from her fingers to land on
the unit, I continued for her. "I pray we can return to
the partnership and trust we once enjoyed."

"He was trying to make peace," whispered Amelia.
"Even after he suspected James was cheating him, he
was still trying to save their friendship."

The date on the letter was just weeks before James
Campbell's suicide. Jeremiah Donovan had been trying
to reconcile with his partner even as Campbell was
planning to frame him for theft.

"There's another document here," said Amelia,
lifting a receipt from the drawer. "The painting was
delivered to Sarah Campbell after James's death.
Jeremiah must have sent it to his widow anyway, even
after everything that happened."

She laid the scrap of paper on top of the plan
cabinet and carefully smoothed it out, as if this would
somehow achieve the same with the past. "Margaret's
precious family heirloom was a gift from the man she

spent forty years trying to destroy." She gave a heartfelt sigh before whispering, "So much wasted effort."

"The irony is tragic," I agreed.

As we organized the documents, vindication settled over us, although this was interrupted when my phone rang. Not a news alert, but a call from the contact who'd been feeding me information about the federal investigation brewing in the background.

"I need to take this," I said, stepping away from Amelia.

The voice at the other end was cautious. "You need to see the news. It's happening."

After hanging up, I pulled up multiple news sites, my hands trembling as I read the headlines.

"What is it?" asked Amelia.

"It's a trap," I said automatically. "Has to be. They want me to surface, to believe I'm safe, and then..."

"Mal." Her voice was gentle but firm. "Whatever it is, read it again. Slowly."

But I couldn't. The words kept blurring. I couldn't switch off three years of hyper-vigilance because of half-a-dozen random news articles. "They've tried this before. False flag operations, fake news stories designed to flush out assets."

After scoffing at my obvious paranoia, she grabbed my phone and read the articles, taking her time. "These are federal arrests, Mal. Public record. Real charges, real names."

I wanted to believe her. God, I wanted to believe her so much. But the instincts that had kept me alive for three years screamed that this was too convenient, too perfect.

"No, Lia, those are the bastards who burned me," I said, skimming the article again. "The ones who set me up to take the fall for that screwup in Syria. You think they can't threaten the press to print a bunch of lies?"

The three men who'd destroyed my life, who'd forced me to disappear and assume a new identity, were capable of that and more. That justice had finally caught up with them was taking some swallowing.

Not that they were being charged for what they'd done to me, but rather the international incident they'd buried by making me the scapegoat.

"What does this mean?" said Amelia.

"If it's true, it could mean I'm free," I said, hardly daring to hope. "But I can't trust this. Not yet. It's too convenient, too perfect."

"What do you need to do?" Amelia asked quietly.

"Verify everything. Cross-reference records. I need to check multiple sources. It'll take time." I looked at her seriously. "But first, we deal with Margaret. These documents are our priority right now."

She nodded. "One crisis at a time."

The next morning, Chase called his contact at the sheriff's department, turning over the evidence we'd agreed to release. Two days later, the legal turnaround began.

Faced with documented proof that hinted at her ancestor having been the actual criminal, Margaret Quinn's legal team began a rapid retreat. Something I suspected would have involved a lot of screaming and cursing on her part.

The three law firms withdrew their motions without a murmur, the Campbell Historical Preservation Trust dissolved overnight, and Amelia's building permits were restored within twenty-four hours.

It was amazing what some leverage in the form of potential social annihilation could achieve. Especially in a town as small as Coogan's Break.

Margaret herself, when confronted with the evidence of her family's genuine history, suffered what her lawyer called a severe psychological episode, although I'd call it a meltdown. It was one that was dramatic enough to see her transferred from the county jail to a psychiatric facility for evaluation.

The district attorney, emboldened by the clear evidence, expanded her charges to include fraud and racketeering. Margaret was ultimately sentenced to twelve years in federal prison. Her corrupt network dissolved overnight as former allies distanced themselves, leaving her to face the consequences alone.

Even her own family disowned her. Rebecca Quinn-Morrison publicly stated she would donate any inheritance to compensate Margaret's victims, wanting no part of her mother's obsession. Funny that she'd been all for it when she'd agreed to have her name linked to the historical society.

"Forty years of hatred based on a lie," said Amelia as we stood in the warehouse basement three days later, looking at the hole where we'd found Campbell's original hidden cache. "She destroyed herself chasing a fantasy."

"The truth has a way of coming out in the end," I replied, pulling her close. "Question is, what do you want to do now?"

As we made our way back up to the main floor, she looked around the warehouse that had caused so much pain and obsession, her expression one of peace.

"The cops can deal with Margaret and her family, but I've decided I don't want to press charges. I refuse to let that woman's spite contaminate me. Rather, I want to finish what I started," she said, turning around so she could take everything in.

"I want to turn this place into something beautiful. Not through public spectacle, but through simple acknowledgment of the truth. Something that tells the true story. Jeremiah's story."

"Including the gold?"

"Especially the gold. But replicas in a display case, not the real thing. I'm not crazy enough to start another gold rush." She leaned into my warmth before continuing. "The treasure is the truth. People should know what kind of man Jeremiah Donovan was."

"And what about us?" I asked. "What's our truth?"

She looked up at me with those dark eyes that had become my anchor through everything. "Our truth is that we make a good team. In this building, with the crew, and whatever comes next."

"I can live with that," I said, but there was something else I needed to say. "Amelia, I want you to know I'm not going anywhere. This isn't just about the building anymore, or about Margaret Quinn. This is about us."

"I know," she whispered. "I feel it too."

"When I thought about losing you when you were taken. It scared me more than anything I'd faced in my old life. Because you're not just someone I'm protecting anymore. You're my partner. In everything."

She reached up and wrapped her hands around the back of my neck. "Partners," she agreed. "In everything."

Looking around the basement where it all started, I could see the future taking shape. The warehouse would be restored, better than ever. The gold discovery would become part of its history, drawing visitors who'd learn about the real Jeremiah Donovan. A man who'd tried to do right even when wronged.

And Amelia and I would build something lasting together. A partnership based on trust, truth, and the sort of love that could survive anything.

We'd proven that some legacies were worth fighting for. Some truths were worth uncovering. And while our modern-day gold rush was over, what we'd found together was more valuable than anything James Campbell had ever stolen.

In the weeks that followed, as the warehouse project moved forward, I worked quietly to verify the federal arrests. It took painstaking investigation, including cross-referencing records, checking multiple sources, and having Chase's contacts confirm details through law enforcement channels.

The hardest part was learning to trust that freedom might actually be possible, that after three years of running and hiding, it was time to take risks.

And Amelia? For her, I'd risk it all.

EPILOGUE

SIX MONTHS LATER

AMELIA

Standing at the heart of the renovated Donovan Warehouse, watching the final preparations for the grand opening, I was filled with a sense of wonder that still took my breath away.

The transformation was stunning. The original stone walls had been restored with love and skill, their golden patina catching the light from the new fixtures we'd installed throughout the space. The ground floor housed six artisan studios, each one already buzzing with creative energy.

Perhaps my biggest coup in this area was signing local glass artist Macie Hart, coaxing her out of her home studio for a couple of days each week. Such was her fame that I knew there'd be people lined up around the block whenever she released a new season's jewelry.

It had helped immensely that Macie was married to Brad McKenna, who also worked for Lucky Break Construction.

Looking back, I marveled at the woman I'd become. The Amelia who'd first walked into this warehouse would never have had the confidence to approach someone like Macie Hart, much less convince her to partner with an untested venture. But transformation wasn't a destination. It was a daily choice to choose courage over comfort, growth over safety.

Every risk I'd taken had paid off, but more importantly, each leap of faith had revealed more of who I truly was beneath all those careful layers of protection. Funny, but in renovating the warehouse, I'd also renovated myself.

The loft apartments upstairs were occupied but for one, their enormous windows offering spectacular views of Coogan's Break and the California coast in both directions.

But the crown jewel was the historical exhibit we'd created in the basement, celebrating Jeremiah Donovan's legacy. The display cases held crafted replicas of the gold we'd found, along with reproductions of documents that showed Jeremiah's character, including his meticulous business records.

"The caterers are asking about the timeline for speeches," said Malakai, appearing at my elbow with two glasses of champagne.

I accepted the bubbles with gratitude, still awed at how natural it felt to have this handsome man at my side. Okay, and I couldn't help but drool over how gorgeous he looked in his new dark charcoal suit. Perhaps the biggest change was that he was clean shaven, the handlebar mustache he'd hidden behind all those years now gone.

He scrubbed up well, this man of mine.

This man of mine?

That was something else I was still marveling over. Finding my soul mate hadn't been on my punch list when I arrived in Coogan's Break to tackle the renovation. And yet, it was my biggest achievement to date.

After taking a sip of his champagne, Mal tipped his head toward the kitchen area. "It would appear that the woman running the show is a bit of a perfectionist."

"You're right. Nadia Becker runs a tight ship," I agreed, looking at the curvy event coordinator in her monogrammed navy jumpsuit. Despite a ready smile, the woman was managing every detail with military precision.

"She seems to know what she's doing," observed Malakai, before breaking into a grin so broad it transformed his entire face. "Although I think our boy Daemon might be a little distracted by more than just her professional competence."

I followed his gaze to where Daemon was making out that he was helping move chairs, but was just finding excuses to linger near where Nadia was working. Every time she gave instructions to her staff, he'd try to catch her eye. When she stretched over to adjust the centerpiece that crowned the round table in the main foyer, his attention was not on the floral arrangement.

"He's not subtle, is he?" I laughed, although not at him. There was a fragility to Daemon that I'd missed when I first met him. Easy enough to do given his bravado, and a face made even more attractive by the scars of his shady past.

"About as subtle as a brick through a window," agreed Malakai. "But I have to give him credit for persistence. She's shot down every attempt he's made to ask her out so far, and he just keeps coming back for more."

"Maybe he's met his match," I suggested, watching as Nadia sidestepped Daemon's latest attempt at conversation while directing two servers and checking something on her tablet.

"Could be interesting," said Malakai. "The irresistible force meets the immovable object."

"Speaking of interesting," I said, spotting the first guests arriving through the main entrance, "I think we're about to launch this thing."

The evening was everything I'd dreamed of and more. The warehouse was filled with laughter, conversation, and the warm glow of success. Local dignitaries mingled with artists, the Lucky Break crew chatted with my team from the Redding office, and everyone seemed delighted by what we'd accomplished.

As I'd hoped, the historical exhibition was the biggest hit, with people clustered around the display cases, reading all about what an upstanding citizen Jeremiah Donovan had been. As tempting as it was to do a hatchet job on James Campbell, I'd resisted, for fear it would leave a poor impression.

And it had been the right choice, with several visitors mentioning they were already planning return trips to bring friends and family. They wouldn't have done that if I'd outright accused one of the town's founding fathers of a felony.

"You did it," said Ethan, raising his beer in a toast as the Lucky Break crew and their partners gathered near the bar we'd set up in the main gallery. "This place is incredible."

"Not just me," I corrected, looking around at the people who'd become like family. "All of us together."

Tyler nodded toward the basement stairs, where a steady stream of visitors was heading down to see the exhibit. "The gold story will bring tourists from all over the state, I'm sure of it. It's been a while since anyone struck gold."

"The irony would be enough to choke Margaret Quinn," said Cole with dark satisfaction. "All that scheming, and now the building's worth more than she ever imagined."

"I try not to think about her or her rotten family," I said. "This place is about moving forward, not dwelling on the past."

"Good philosophy," said Malakai, his arm settling around my waist in a gesture that had become as natural as breathing.

All too soon, the last guests filtered out, and Nadia's team began clearing away the remnants of the celebration. I noticed Daemon making one last attempt to engage her in conversation, but she was all business, checking items off her list and directing her staff with brisk professionalism.

"Another time, Mr. Booth," she said, when he

suggested drinks to celebrate. "It's been a long day, and there's still much to do."

As she continued to supervise her team and help where necessary, Daemon watched her, his expression that of a man who'd just been presented with his greatest challenge yet.

"She's got his number," observed Tyler with amusement.

"Good," said Cole. "Someone needs to keep that boy humble."

"She needs to be careful. During planning, she let me know she's got family who depend on her. Plus, her business reputation matters in a town this size. I doubt she'd risk those with the likes of Daemon."

Much as I liked him, Mal wasn't wrong when he called the guy a man whore.

After the caterers had finished and everyone else had headed home, I found myself alone with Malakai in the transformed space that had brought us together. The warehouse felt different now. Not just because of the renovation, but because of everything we'd been through to get here.

"Come with me," I said, taking his hand. "There's something I want to show you."

I led him up to the top floor, to Jeremiah's restored office where we'd made love that golden afternoon and discovered the hidden drawer. The room was now part of the premium loft apartment.

"Remember this place?" I asked, running my hand along the plan drawer unit that had played such a crucial role in our story.

"How could I forget?" said Malakai, his voice rough with memory. "This is where everything changed."

"And it's where everything begins," I said, reaching into my pocket and pulling out a brass key tied with a red ribbon. "This is yours."

He looked confused. "What's this?"

"The key to this place." I pressed it into his hands. "I know you've been living in that fortress of yours for security reasons, but now that your past is behind you... I thought you might like to come home. To a proper home."

His eyes filled with understanding. "Lia..."

"And you can't say the security isn't foolproof. You designed it yourself. And I can't think of anyone more deserving of living where the truth was finally discovered." I smiled. "Besides, I'd like to wake up next to the man I love in our home, not just visit him in his safe house."

He stared at the key for a long moment, then pulled me close. "Our home," he said, voice rough with emotion. "I like the sound of that."

Then, before I could lose my nerve, I struggled out

of his embrace and hit the trigger mechanism, with the hidden drawer popping open. Malakai's eyes went wide with shock when I retrieved the small velvet box I'd hidden there earlier that day.

"Malakai Torres," I said, my voice steady despite my racing heart, "you walked into my life when I needed you most. You helped me fight for my family's legacy and build something beautiful. You've been my partner from the moment we met, and I want you at my side for everything to come." After dropping to one knee, I flipped the lid of the small box and held it out to him. "Will you marry me?"

The look on his face was worth every nervous moment I'd spent planning this. Surprise, joy, and something deeper that took my breath away.

"Jesus, Amelia," he said, before dropping to his knees to meet me at eye level. "Are you proposing to me?"

"I'm a modern woman," I said with a grin. "I go after what I want. And I want you. Forever."

"Then yes," he said, gripping my hands and the small box as if his life depended on it. "Yes, to everything. To marriage, to partnership, to whatever comes next. As long as it's with you."

The ring was perfect. A simple platinum band that matched his practical, straightforward nature. As I slipped it onto his finger, he pulled me into a kiss that tasted of champagne and promises yet to be fulfilled.

"I love you," I whispered against his lips.

"I love you, too," he replied. "More than I ever thought possible."

As we held each other, I could hear the city settling into evening around us. The warehouse that had been empty and forgotten for so long was now alive with purpose, filled with dreams and possibilities.

We'd restored more than just a building. We'd restored truth, justice, and faith in the power of love to overcome any obstacle. The gold rush might be over, but what Malakai and I had found together was priceless.

MALAKAI

Looking at Amelia kneeling before me with that ring box, proposing to me in the place where we'd first found the truth about her family, I felt something settle deep in my chest. Something I'd never expected to feel again after losing everything in my old life.

Home. Belonging. A future worth fighting for.

"You realize I had my own plans for tonight," I said, helping her to her feet and wrapping my arms around her. "I've been carrying around my grandmother's ring for three weeks, waiting for the right moment."

Her eyes widened. "You were going to propose to me?"

"Great minds," I said, pulling the antique ring from my pocket.

She laughed, holding out her left hand so I could slip the delicate vintage ring onto her finger. The diamonds caught the light streaming through the windows, and I thought about how my grandmother would have loved Amelia. Would have appreciated her strength, her determination to fight for what mattered.

"Tell me about her," Amelia whispered, studying the ring.

"Elena Garcia. She came to this country with nothing but determination and a sewing machine. Built a life, married my grandfather, raised three kids, became a widow too young." I traced the ring with my thumb. "She always said the right woman would know this ring was meant for her. I never understood what she meant until I met you."

"She sounds incredible."

"She was. And she would have adored you." I pulled Amelia closer, looking around the room that had become so significant to us. "You know what she would have said about all this? About your taking over a falling-down building and turning it into something beautiful?"

"What?"

"Malakai, that's a woman who knows how to build a legacy."

Amelia's eyes filled with tears. "I wish I could have met her."

"She's here," I said, touching the ring. "Part of her, anyway. Just like Jeremiah's still within these walls, in the truth we uncovered."

We stood there for a moment, surrounded by the ghosts of the past and the promise of the future. Six months ago, I'd been a man without a true identity, without a proper home, without hope. Now I had two of the three, wrapped up in the woman in my arms and the community that I'd finally accepted as family.

Whether I'd ever reclaim my birth name, that was a challenge for another day.

"What happens now?" asked Amelia. "We've put rings on it, the warehouse is thriving, Margaret Quinn is where she belongs..."

"Now we live," I said. "We work. We build something together that's bigger than either of us could create alone."

"The warehouse is just the beginning, isn't it?"

I nodded, taking in the lights of Coogan's Break spreading below us. "After the success of the warehouse, Ethan has more jobs than he knows what to do with, which will keep me busy. And there's your consulting on that hotel renovation in Sacramento."

"Partners in business and life," she mused.

"The best kind." I kissed her forehead. "Though I have to warn you, marrying me means you're stuck with the Lucky Break crew for life. They come with the package."

"I wouldn't have it any other way. As you said, they're family."

Family. The word still felt strange sometimes, but it was getting easier. Ethan and the rest of the team had proven to me that family wasn't just about blood. It was about the people who showed up when things got tough, who had your back when your world fell apart, who celebrated your victories like they were their own.

"There's something else," I said, remembering the call I'd received that morning. "Remember those contacts going dark? My former handler was arrested yesterday. It's finally over."

"What does that mean for you?"

"It means I'm free. No one's coming after me anymore. Are you prepared for that?"

She smiled, her eyes sparkling with joy. "I can handle that because I've got big plans."

"I'm sure you do. You always have plans."

"Starting with a wedding," she confirmed. "I'm thinking of something simple here in the warehouse. Nothing fancy, just family and friends."

"Sounds perfect." I paused, struck by a thought.

"You know what's funny? When I first walked into this place six months ago, I thought it was just another job. Another building to secure, another client to protect."

"And now?" she asked.

"Now it's home. It's proof that the truth always surfaces. Jeremiah would be proud of you."

"I know he would be. His story finally has the ending it deserved."

After spinning her around in an impromptu dance, I leaned forward and kissed her forehead. Her lips would soon follow, but for now this was enough.

"For me, it wasn't about protecting the building at all. It was about protecting you. About finding my place and discovering that the best treasures hide in the most unlikely places."

She laughed, the sound echoing off the stone walls. "Are you comparing me to buried gold, Mr. Torres?"

"I'm saying you're worth more than all of James Campbell's stolen treasure combined, Ms. Donovan."

"Soon to be Mrs. Torres," she said, her laughter wrapping around us.

"Could you live with Mrs. Tremaine?"

She repeated it, testing the sound. "I can definitely live with that."

Taking hold of Amelia's hand, I started for the main stairs, eager to get her home and into bed. But she had other ideas.

"We can stay here tonight," she said, pulling me toward the bedroom of the premium apartment. "I figured if you said yes that we wouldn't want to waste time about driving back to your place."

She then opened the bedroom door with a flourish to reveal a room dominated by a four-poster bed and lit candles. There was also no missing the basket of toys on the bedside table.

Never in a million years could I have chosen a better partner. She was perfect for me and the sooner I had her screaming my name, the better.

THANK YOU

If you've enjoyed this story, we'd be thrilled if you could take the time to give it a rating, or even a review, before you leave. In the meantime, carry on to read more about what's coming up next.

Many thanks
The Chicks at Bad Birds

ALL ABOUT HOPE

Hope believes everyone deserves love, especially curvy girls. She also likes to believe there's a welcoming town like Coogan's Break for all of us. A place where the girls are confident and the guys hotter than hell, where opposites attract, and love is steamy and fast.

www.thepapersparrow.com

LUCKY BREAK SERIES

Meet the **Lucky Break Construction** crew, whose motto should read ***"If we build it, you will come!"*** because apparently a few Coogan's Break single ladies have done just that.

www.ingramcontent.com/pod-product-compliance
Lightning Source LLC
Chambersburg PA
CBHW010738310726
48971CB00010B/2876